Never had a man wanted her so much...

Molly couldn't deny the thrill that shot through her when she could so clearly see the urgency in Cam's eyes.

His gaze traveled across her face and down her body.

"I want to do everything at once." And then he had her in his arms, pressed up close, his mouth on hers in a heartbeat.

To think they could have been tangling in the sheets long before tonight...

God, she didn't want to part for a second. Not when it felt this good. When she'd been so afraid of having this moment.

Why had she ever thought that sex with Cam was a bad idea?

Now, though, she was lost in taste and touch. His hands on her back, holding her close, the way he teased her tongue into following his.

He broke away, gasping. "Clothes," he said. "Bed."

Then he stripped off his shirt in one swipe, before kissing her again.

His hands moved to her buttons, which he took care of with such alacrity she wondered if he was a pianist, or if he did card tricks.

But when he kissed the tops of her breasts as he pushed the blouse from her shoulders, she no longer cared.

D0557495

Blaze®

Dear Reader,

Here's a toast to *Dare Me,* book five in the It's Trading Men! series.

Molly Grainger is a wine critic. Cameron Crawford is a brewmaster. Molly knows from the moment she chooses his Hot Guys Trading Card that they're perfect for each other...as long as he doesn't mind that her career is her first priority, and she doesn't mind that his stay in Manhattan is almost over. No, both of them agree that having perfect no-strings-attached hotter-than-hot sex is a fantastic plan. Or it would be, if they weren't falling madly in love!

I love to hear from readers! You can find me @Jo_Leigh, and at tumblr.com/blog/joleighwrites.

Look for my next It's Trading Men! book, *Intrigue Me,* in October!

Happy reading,

Jo Leigh

Dare Me

—

Jo Leigh

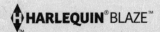

Recycling programs
for this product may
not exist in your area.

ISBN-13: 978-0-373-79812-4

DARE ME

Printed in U.S.A.

ABOUT THE AUTHOR

Jo Leigh is from Los Angeles and always thought she'd end up living in Manhattan. So how did she end up in Utah in a tiny town with a terrible internet connection being bossed around by a house full of rescued cats and dogs? What the heck, she says, predictability is boring. Jo has written more than forty-five novels for Harlequin. Visit her website at www.joleigh.com or contact her at joleigh@joleigh.com.

Books by Jo Leigh

HARLEQUIN BLAZE

To get the inside scoop on Harlequin Blaze and its talented writers, be sure to check out blazeauthors.com.

COSMO RED-HOT READS FROM HARLEQUIN
DEFINITELY NAUGHTY

All backlist available in ebook format.

To Becca and Tiani for the light they've brought
into my life.

1

"OH, COME ON," Emmy said, hands on her hips, looking disappointed when she should be looking guilty.

Cameron Crawford checked the temperature of the mash for The Four Sisters' newest summer ale. Eric Strand, the brewery manager, and his crew were attending to the fermentation tanks and Emmy was being a pain in Cameron's ass, so he ignored her. Until he couldn't hold on to his temper for another second. "You're actually surprised I'm upset that you joined some dating cult thing and used my name and picture without my permission? I know you weren't raised by wolves but only because you're my sister. What the hell were you thinking?"

Emmy narrowed her eyes. "So I should just tear this card up right now."

"Yes," he said. "Please. Do that."

She laughed. He didn't care for the sound of it. "You might be a brainiac chemist with a *doctorate,* little brother, but sometimes you're as dumb as a box of rocks."

That made him turn on her. "Really? A box of rocks?"

"Yes. This is a Hot Guys Trading Card," she said, waving the evidence of her crime as if it were a victory flag.

"Although why I ever considered you being a hot guy is anyone's guess."

He finished the temperature check, made the notes on the log, then moved on. At least it was cold in the brewery, unlike the rest of Queens. The summers continued to get hotter, which meant their utility bills were out of control, but the heat brought a ton of customers to the brewpub. "Right. Let me get this straight. I'm ugly and stupid and…"

"Selfish."

He loved his family, he really did, but it was a lot easier when they weren't living in the same town. All he wanted to do was finish his rounds, then get back to his lab in the back room. "Selfish."

"You should be glad I'm not moping over my divorce. And there's no safer way to find a decent man in this city than Hot Guys Trading Cards."

"Go ahead. Do your trading-card thing all you want. Although, for the record, it doesn't sound safe. But don't make me out to be the bad guy just because I'm sick of you and everyone else playing matchmaker."

"It is safe. Because the men are all direct referrals. Not even friends of friends. You have to know a guy, be related to a guy or work directly with a guy to submit his name. And this has nothing to do with fixing you up. I swear."

"Right."

She glared at him. "I wasn't allowed to choose a card until I'd submitted two of my own."

"First of all," he said, after digesting that bit of information, "you should have led with that, but it still doesn't excuse you from not asking me first."

"I figured you'd want to help me find someone. And honestly…even though it wasn't my intention—" holding up her hands, she backed away "—this could end up being good for you, too."

And there it was again. The big issue. "Just couldn't help yourself, could you?" He shook his head. "Emmy, you know how I feel about setups—I don't like them. I'll meet the right person when it's meant to be. It's all a matter of chemistry, and you can't manufacture that. I believe in serendipity. Not being auctioned off to the highest bidder."

"It's not an auction. You get chosen. If you're lucky. Then she'll call you and you can find out all about her from me, because if I don't know her, I'll at least know some of her friends, and it's likely we'll already have talked before she takes out her cell phone, so yes, it's *safe*. And there's nothing that says serendipity can't happen via a trading card."

"How many women are we talking about here?"

Emmy raised her *I'm so superior* eyebrow, making him regret the question. "At the moment, twenty-seven."

He knew he was going to be sorry, but the prospect of twenty-seven women deserved a little more investigation. "Are they all as old as you?"

"Very funny, you bastard. Keep making comments like that and I really will tear up the card."

With great self-control, he faced his sister head-on, deciding the quickest way out was to let her have her say. "Fine. What kind of young ladies are they?"

"Single working women. Our group meets near my office, so most of them work in the East Village. And so far, everyone's been really nice. Mindy—you know, my friend from krav maga—she invited me."

"I have no idea who you're talking about."

"It doesn't matter. She's been to the bar plenty of times, but anyway—" Emmy took a step closer to him. "Wait a minute. She was here last Friday night and you talked to her for, like, twenty minutes. Blonde? Green eyes? Talks like she's from Jersey?"

"You talk like you're from Jersey."

"I do not."

"Wait, Mindy? I think I remember her now," he said. "Shorter than you, right?"

"Good try. Everyone's shorter than me."

He shrugged. Even twenty-seven single women wasn't worth much more of this. He'd come back six months ago to help his dad with the craft-beer business. The first four months, he'd been neck-deep in work, so his sisters had left him alone. But lately the whole meddling bunch had been trying to set him up with friends, acquaintances… bar customers… That was the worst. At least Emmy wasn't pressing him to get married before he left Queens. Probably because she was the only one in the family to have been through a divorce.

Emmy must have realized she was losing him, because her voice got softer. "Okay, look, we're not dummies. We know we're throwing women at you, but you know why. It's Dad. He lives for the day you find a woman like Mom. At least with the trading cards, you've got a chance of meeting someone who doesn't live in the neighborhood."

"I'll only be here a few more months, and I'd really appreciate some time off from work and setups. I do just fine on my own in Syracuse, so why does everyone think I need so much help?" He frowned at the card. "What's all that writing on the back?" he asked, holding out his hand.

She pulled the card away. "You're gonna thank me."

"Not feeling the gratitude yet."

"It says you're a brewmaster."

His first instinct was to correct her, but she wasn't wrong. Not exactly. "Why didn't you say I'm a chemist?" he asked, his hand still sticking out, waiting. "Since that's what I am."

"Because women don't think of sex when you say *chemist*."

"And they do when you say *brewmaster?*"

She just smiled. "I also said your favorite restaurant is Prune."

"Prune? It is not." He made a grab for the card, but damn all six feet of her, she was quick.

"I know. But if I put down your favorite restaurant is White Castle, no one would ever want to date you."

Not that he'd tell her, but she might have had a point. Although to be clear, White Castle burgers were only one of his favorite foods. He also loved pizza. "Is that it? That's everything on the card?"

"Nope. I also said your secret passion was creating prize-winning beer, that you're not nearly as nerdy as you sound, that you're an all-around great guy, and—"

"You called me a nerd?"

"And all-around great guy."

"Yeah. Thanks a bunch. Now can I see it?"

She smiled too quickly. "Sure," she said, handing it over. "Good picture, huh?"

"I don't remember this photo."

"Because Jade took it. Stealthily."

"Great. Now it's not just one sister. It's a conspiracy."

"You might want to turn the card over, Narcissus, and take a look. At each response."

His sigh said exactly what he thought about what she'd put down for him. Until he got to the choice of marry, date or one-night stand. Ah. Okay. So Emmy *did* get the only thing he was interested in. "Fine," he said, handing back the card. "I'll do it. But only because I'm a good brother."

Her laughter followed him all the way across the brewery until he closed the door behind him.

"GOLDFISH," MOLLY GRAINGER SAID, leaning slightly away from the microphone that dangled in front of her face. "I assume you mean the crackers, not the actual fish."

Her "frequent listener, first-time caller" Andy laughed. "Yeah. The crackers. The Hot 'n Spicy Cheddar ones."

"Give me a second." Although she already knew the wine she'd recommend, Molly waited a few beats for dramatic effect. "Malbec," she said. "Definitely a Malbec. And I suggest trying one from Argentina. They've done wonderful things with an often neglected grape."

"Okay," Andy said. "But what makes it good to drink with Goldfish?"

"It stands up well to strong flavors. Malbec has a jammy character, and a great blend of aromas and flavors that makes it very complex, so you're not just putting out the fire, but adding to the dining experience. Plus there are some very good choices for under twenty-five bucks. Let me know what you think."

"Cool. *Gracias.*"

"De nada," she said, then added, "This is Molly Grainger and you're listening to *Molly's Wine for Newbies* on WNYU radio. We'll be right back."

She clicked off her mike and switched her attention to the card that was sitting on her console. She'd just come back from her fifth Hot Guys Trading Cards meeting, and for the first time ever she'd selected a guy. His name was Cameron Crawford. Although he was, by any standard, a very good-looking man, she'd chosen him because he was a brewmaster, a distant cousin of sorts, careerwise. That should make the small talk easier.

Fact was, while she'd worked for years to overcome her natural shyness in order to teach and speak in public, she still had a hard time with personal one-on-one conversations. Which shouldn't have mattered, since there was no room in her life for anything but a one-night stand right now, and yet she wasn't about to jump in the sack without at least finding out if she liked the guy first.

Her being a master sommelier and well on her way to becoming a master of wine and Cameron's passion for brewing gave them enough in common to begin a conversation without too much flailing about. And after meeting his sister Emerald, Molly doubted he'd be horrid. Emmy seemed bright and funny and had that very enviable ability to fit in with a broad assortment of people.

Now all that was left was for Molly to call Cameron and set up a time and place for dinner. Somewhere that wasn't Prune. She was going to foot the tab, and there was no way she wanted to pay those kinds of prices. She'd already learned that he lived in Queens, so she focused her restaurant search on the area around the Queensboro Bridge. Bistango's, perhaps, or Tommy Bahama.

But before she dialed Cameron's number, she called the woman who'd introduced her to the trading cards: Donna, her boss at *Wine Connoisseur* and her closest friend. Molly's producer, Roxanne, would signal her a few seconds before they went back on the air.

Donna answered on the first ring. "Did you call him yet?"

"Nope." Jeez. Donna had been with her when she'd chosen the card all of one hour ago. "But I've figured out where I want to meet. The problem is what happens after."

Donna was silent for a second. "It's a date, Mol. You've been on dates."

"Yes, thank you for being so literal." Molly studied his card again. "He lives all the way out in Queens. You think he's going to want to come all the way to Bensonhurst for a one-off?" Donna's laugh was so loud, Molly had to move her phone away from her ear.

"You think a guy looking for a one-night stand via a trading card is gonna balk at a train ride? You have been celibate for way too long."

"It's not celibacy if you don't have time for it."

"Were you having sex? No? That's being celibate in my book. You've been so busy working I doubt you've seen one movie this whole year. Am I right? Of course I'm right. You need to call this man."

"I'm calling him! Stop yelling at me. I just... I wouldn't go to Queens for him. That's all."

"He won't mind. I promise."

"Hey, Molly. You can screw at my place." Bobby's voice boomed over the intercom.

Molly closed her eyes. She'd neglected to cut off the intercom between her and the booth. When she did look, it was with a glare at the engineer. "I'm one hundred percent certain you've hooked up your entire apartment with video cameras," Molly said. "You're a perv, Bobby!" Turning her attention back to Donna, she said, "I'll call you after I set things up."

Donna said, "Good," then hung up just as Bobby said, "I'm a guy, Molly. Did you know we think about sex every six seconds? My interest in the subject is a biological imperative."

"Your interest in the subject is that you can't keep it in your pants," Roxanne said, her voice dripping with disdain. Theirs was not a match made in heaven. Shockingly, Bobby looked a little ashamed. Not that it would last.

Molly couldn't have been happier that Roxanne had joined their team as a producer. Molly had originally worked with a guy named Wesley, who not only didn't understand wine, but hadn't understood the basics of personal hygiene. University radio stations were great, but the constant revolving door of personnel was a crapshoot.

"In three…two…" Roxanne gave Molly the signal. Her next caller had obviously taken a cue from the caller before the break and wanted to know what wine to pair with popcorn.

"Buttered?"

"Why not?" the caller asked.

Again, Molly went to the base ingredients, the underlying flavors and texture of the food. Popcorn was, after all, corn. And the butter meant she needed something sharp enough to cut the coating sensation on the tongue. "There's a nice aromatic wine called Viognier that would fit the bill." She spelled the word, which she had to do with a number of wines. "It's a reasonably priced white—at least, the California varieties are. Look for Cold Heaven, and make sure the bottle's well chilled. Then enjoy the movie."

The requests continued in that vein for the next fifteen minutes. One ridiculous pairing after another. Molly ended up pleased with the hour. They'd had a lot of calls. She was so happy that she did some extra commercial recordings before she gathered her briefcase, her phone and her notes for the following week's show and headed out to make the all-important phone call to Mr. Crawford.

But first she borrowed Roxanne's empty office to steal a few minutes alone with her tablet. Molly checked her messages, texted a few replies and then went to her calendar. It was a masterpiece of organization born of necessity. Every day of the month was broken down into half-hour segments, and each segment was tied to her agenda, including breaks for meals, phone conversations that might take longer than five minutes, blogging, teaching, wine tasting, writing, editing… The list went on. What she was looking for now was evenings when she was free. She usually ended up sleeping or working on her evenings off. Occasionally she'd read, but mostly for research. In the past six months, she'd met Donna for drinks three times.

Ever since she'd gone to her first trading-cards meeting—ironically in the basement at St. Marks Church—she'd been shifting her schedule just enough to clear two possible nights next week when she could meet her date, have a meal or a drink, have sex and make it back to her apartment before one the next morning.

She found them on the following Thursday and Sunday. Granted, it would have been better if she'd blocked out a Friday or Saturday night, but those tended to get booked up months in advance with wine tastings, lectures, classes. She had an all-expenses-paid four-day event coming up in the Hamptons, and she'd had to do some serious reshuffling to attend that.

She dialed the number on the card, her heart beating rapidly, her mouth dry as a desert until her call went directly to voice mail.

Cameron sounded nice. And sexy. And polite when he asked her to leave a message.

"Hi, this is Molly Grainger. I'm calling about your trading card. I'd like to talk to you about meeting for a drink next week. I'm into wine as a career, and you're into beer, so…give me a call." She left her phone number and cut the connection, hoping she hadn't sounded too much as though she wanted to sell him life insurance. But at least it was done. He'd probably call. Just hopefully not while she was stuck in a sardine sandwich on the subway going home.

She'd just made it out of the building when Bobby came jogging up to her. He was dressed in his regular uniform of raggedy jeans and a loud T-shirt, this one declaring his passion for zombies. To be fair, her tailored slacks and starched white blouse were her own version of a uniform. Ever since she'd set her sights on becoming a world-class wine expert, she'd dressed for the part, even back when she hadn't had ten cents to rub together. God bless the Goodwill and consignment stores.

"Hey, Mol, this whole trading-cards thing. Can I get in on that action?"

She didn't even hesitate. She wouldn't wish that upon any poor woman. "Sorry, but no."

"Seriously?" Bobby's breath still carried the distinctive smoky notes of *Cannabis sativa*.

She took a step back. "Seriously."

"Okay." He shrugged. "See you next week."

She stopped for a moment to watch him flirt with a young woman standing outside their building holding an armful of books before he went back inside. Had Molly ever been that relaxed, that young? Sometimes it felt as if she'd spent most of her life on a treadmill, running as fast as possible and gaining little ground. But that wasn't completely true. At twenty-seven she'd already accomplished so much. As long as she stayed on track, there was nothing but success ahead of her.

Which reminded her...it was four-fifteen already, and she had a wine-tasting class at six, which meant she just had time to make it home for a quick shower and change before she had to be at Winesby to do her setup. She'd given the kitchen at the restaurant and wine shop the menu before the classes had begun. Tonight's tasting was Focus on Red, which she particularly loved.

She made it onto the D train in the nick of time. Not surprisingly, she didn't score a seat, but she wasn't so squished that she couldn't steal another glance at Cameron's trading card. A brewmaster. A great-looking brewmaster with wavy dark hair, sinfully dark eyes and a mischievous smile. Okay, if he called while she was on the train, she wouldn't answer. She'd wait. Call him back on her own time. The idea of finding someone she could actually talk to while they were in bed was proving to be very enticing. She just hoped he would be free on Sunday or Thursday, because she honestly didn't think she could make it much longer with just her vibrator and fantasies of Benedict Cumberbatch to get her through.

2

As HARD AS the air conditioner at Bistango's tried, it couldn't keep up with the entry area. The summer sun was still out at seven, and the heat followed everyone who walked in.

Cameron hadn't been to the restaurant in years, but he was happy to be back. Especially when it meant meeting someone who sounded so interesting. Ever since Molly had called to set up the date, he'd become a little too invested in the outcome. Although he knew he shouldn't get ahead of himself. One-night stand didn't necessarily mean same-night stand.

But he hoped it would.

One more glance at the door, and there she was. She was prettier than the pictures on her website, and those had been damn good. He hadn't realized she'd be so slim. That wasn't even the right word. *Delicate* was more accurate. Five-seven or so, auburn hair that curved and swirled across her shoulders, and big dark eyes that might have captured every bit of his attention if it hadn't been for her figure.

Online, she'd appeared trim and sophisticated. What the photographs had failed to show were her curves.

"Cameron," she said, holding out her hand. Her handshake was firm, and her gaze roamed down to his chest before it came back up to meet his eyes. "Molly Grainger," she said. "I hope you haven't been waiting long."

"Nope. Just got here myself." Neither of them had let go yet. "Nice to meet you, Molly. You can call me Cam." She had one of those smiles that made him automatically grin in return. "Well, I guess I'll go check on our reservation."

He nodded toward a brunette holding menus. "The hostess is waiting for us."

"Oh, good."

Walking slightly behind her, he stole a glance at her round, pert bottom and slender legs. Things had gone from good to great, and they hadn't even talked yet. After weaving their way through the dinner crowd, they were seated in a relatively private booth.

Molly stared at him for longer than he was expecting, but it wasn't the eyes-meet-and-linger of a sexual connection. More of an *oh, God, what have I done?* look.

"I was impressed with your website," Cam said, hoping to ease her discomfort. "I read some of your articles. Very interesting. Our professions dovetail in so many areas."

"My website?" Her shoulders sagged on a sigh. "Oh."

Cam's grin faded. "Is that against the rules or something?"

"What? No, of course not. It's just—" She straightened. Her shoulders were neatly squared by a white blouse that looked old-fashioned to him, but then again, he knew nothing about trends. Besides, who cared when she was so pretty. "So much for making small talk. You already know everything about me."

"Somehow I doubt that. Unless all you do is work."

"Basically, that is all I do, yes."

"So that explains why someone so attractive is doing the trading-card thing."

Her cheeks turned a little pinker. "And what's your excuse?"

"A meddling sister."

Molly raised her eyebrows. "So you don't actually want to be here."

"No, no, no. I didn't say that. In fact, I can't think of any place I'd rather be." He meant it. Whether it was just nerves or something else, he could tell she was struggling to hold her reactions in check, but, in fact, she was very expressive. Fascinatingly so. Even now, the blush that had been on the apples of her cheeks was spreading to her temples. "Which doesn't mean my sister didn't meddle. She's a first-class buttinsky. Her and the rest of my sisters…and, damn, I just remembered that you know her."

"Don't worry about it. We've met, but I wouldn't say I know her."

"Thank God. She's a lot stronger than she looks."

They exchanged smiles, and just before he was going to ask her if she'd gone on these kinds of dates before, he was interrupted by the waitress requesting their drink orders. Molly asked for a few more minutes so she could decide on her meal first, and Cam got a little excited. If she didn't want to linger over cocktails, maybe that meant they were headed on the fast track to the bedroom. The menu suddenly seemed more interesting. Couldn't go wrong with a steak. Good source of protein. If he was lucky, he'd need the stamina later. "Any idea what you're going to get?"

She looked up as he set his menu aside. "I was thinking of ordering the baby-artichoke antipasti with a house salad. What would you recommend pairing with it?"

"Isn't that your specialty?" he asked, surprised, hoping it wasn't a test. He knew what he liked, but he was a novice when it came to wine.

"It is, yes, but I'll be having beer tonight. I'm off the clock."

He liked the way she'd leaned in to tell him that bit. As if being off the clock was a special treat. After seeing her work calendar on her website, he could understand why.

"Let me take a look." He grabbed his menu again. "I haven't been here in a while and I don't know what they're serving anymore." It took him a minute to focus on the liquor selections instead of Molly. The beer list wasn't extensive, but the offerings were excellent. "If you're game, I'd go with the Green Flash. It's a great India pale ale, really complex flavors and strong hops."

The smile he got in response was a knockout. "I'm game. That's one I've never tried, and it sounds excellent."

After the waitress had taken their orders, Molly turned to him again, crossing her arms on the wooden table as she leaned in. "Now that we have that settled, I'm anxious to hear about you. You're my first hot guy."

Glad he hadn't been drinking, he stifled a cough. "Uh…"

"I mean, first trading-card guy. I've met hot men before."

"Well, you're my first trading-card woman, so we're even."

"Fair enough," she said, "but none of that gets you out of telling me about your life. I know you make craft beers and that you come from a tall family. Your turn."

"You didn't look me up?"

"I can now see my error in judgment regarding that, but no. I didn't. I spoke briefly to Emerald and took a chance on your card."

"All right. I have four sisters, all of them tall and athletic. My family owns a bar in Queens called, strangely enough, The Four Sisters, and you're right. I'm into craft beers."

He could have mentioned the job in Syracuse, but he didn't bother. Besides, he wanted the spotlight back on her.

"Why's it called The Four Sisters? What are you, chopped liver?"

"Ha. I'll have to remember to mention that to Emmy. It got its name before any of my sisters were born. My dad had four sisters. So I guess he's chopped liver, not me."

She grew flushed again. "I just meant—"

"I know," he said, grinning. "Personally, I think it should be changed to One Brother and Four Pains in His Butt, but that might be hard to put on the label."

Giggles like champagne bubbles were made even better by Molly's efforts to stem them. Man, giggles could go bad in so many ways, but hers made him want to be funny for a living.

"For what it's worth, I'd think twice before picking up any beverage that had *butts* on the label. No matter what the context."

"And that's why I stick to creating the beers, not naming them."

The waitress came by with the drinks, and Molly visibly relaxed as she closed her eyes and brought the mug up close.

He found himself sniffing when she did, even though his beer was still on the table. And when she parted her lips to take her first sip, he mimicked the move, hoping like hell she would use that much intensity when they were kissing.

"Oh, yes," she said, except it sounded way too much like something he'd hear in bed.

God, he was in trouble.

"You and I are going to get along well." Molly looked into his eyes, her gaze rapt, a whole new kind of brightness lighting her face. "This is exactly what you promised. A big, juicy hop-forward aroma with citrus and piney hops." Another sip, this one rolled around on her tongue before she swallowed. "Ah. Grapefruit, mango, pineapple. It's difficult to get too much nuance with all the competing smells in the room, but the strength of the hops and pine resin really come through. Delicious."

He wanted to sweep her into his arms and kiss her until morning. Instead, he picked up his lager. "To hops and grapes," he said.

They clinked.

HALFWAY THROUGH HER SALAD, Molly put her fork down. There hadn't been a word spoken between her and Cameron for what had to be two minutes. A completely comfortable two minutes.

On a first date.

With the best-looking man in the restaurant.

He'd worn a short-sleeved shirt, silky gray, that begged to be touched and jeans. Worn jeans. And he'd tucked that silky gray shirt into the worn jeans so that every time she thought of him in a whole-picture sense, it was all about broad shoulders tapering to tight hips and long legs.

She sighed as she took another bite of lettuce. Here was a man who not only understood winespeak, but who made her laugh, whose smile did something wicked to her insides and who'd spent a considerable amount of time asking her questions instead of talking about himself.

Huh.

"What?" Cameron's steak-filled fork hung suspended between his plate and mouth. "Is everything okay?"

She nodded. "Everything's fine. Surprisingly so."

"What do you mean?"

She wondered how much to tell him. This was a very

temporary situation, after all. One of the great things about
the one-night-stand concept was that she didn't have to go
into detail. To think that the easiest thing in her life right
now was having sex with a man whose eyes were the color
of crème de cacao made her feel almost giddy. "I'm usually not so relaxed on a first date."

He shrugged. "You're easy to talk to."

"You'd be surprised. It's better with you because of what
we have in common, I think."

"Maybe," he said. "But after seeing the kind of schedule you keep, I have a feeling you're just grateful there
won't be a test. Is that page on your website real? I mean,
how do you even have time to date? I'm busy, but your
life's insane."

"It's real. Well, it's just a sample, but it's a great visual
aid when I have to turn down social engagements. On the
other hand, most people I know are in the same boat. Everyone's working ridiculous hours, handling more of the
load than is feasible, and so scared to lose their jobs that
they never even think of taking time off. That is, if they're
not spending all day hunting for work."

"I know. Especially in New York. I see that every night
at the bar. We have to be careful about how much we serve
to people, make sure they're not driving home. It used to
be that folks came by to relax, play some pool, taste some
brews. Now a lot of customers come in to get hammered.
It's a problem."

She'd been about to ask for a second beer, but maybe
water was a better option. "At least I'm in charge of my
time. No one else to blame. Besides, it'll all pay off in
the end."

"Which will be…?"

"Becoming a major player in the world of fine wines. I

want to be at the top. I think I can do it, too, if I keep my priorities straight."

"Impressive," he said. "With your drive and ambition, I can see it happening."

"If I don't weaken," she said, hearing the fierceness in her own voice.

He jerked his head back a bit, as if she'd startled him. "There's always something tempting on the horizon. But you clearly love what you do. That's the key. We're lucky. We're both working in fields we're passionate about."

Although he was being really nice about it, she knew she'd gone too far. Sometimes she became too strident, didn't explain herself well. It wasn't always easy for people to understand that she had only herself to rely upon. No sisters to bug her, no thicker-than-water blood ties. So she smiled, relaxed her shoulders. "So, tell me about your brewery."

His eyes lit up. And there was equilibrium again. Damn if she hadn't hit the trading-card jackpot. To celebrate, she threw caution to the wind and ordered them both refills on their beers. He told her all about the new lambic brewing he was trying. She'd never even heard of the process— something about using wild yeasts—but he made it sound fascinating. With every anecdote, every lift of excitement in his strong baritone voice, she liked him more and more.

In fact, her body was having a little fiesta all its own, complete with fireworks that lit her up from the blush on her cheeks to the pressure between her legs. Mr. Crawford had started out the evening being good-looking, but now he was *attractive*.

Maybe ordering more drinks had been a mistake. Still, when was the last time she'd been so caught up in a conversation? She'd hardly given a thought to the busy day she had tomorrow.

"I'm sorry," he said. "I get carried away talking about the brewery. I'd much rather hear about how you managed to become a master sommelier and a master of wine when you're barely old enough to drink."

"You charmer. I'm twenty-seven. And I'm not a master of wine yet. I still have my dissertation to finish before I can claim that title."

"Not the point. I'm no expert, but I know what it takes to get that far. And, what, are you the youngest master sommelier ever?"

"One of. I started early. I had two terrific mentors, both deeply involved in the business, to help me along. Simone grew up at her family's vineyard in France, and Phillip is also a master of wine and runs a very successful international wine distribution company. I happen to love the taste and I have a decent nose and palate, so they took me under their wing. With their support, I got lucky."

"I don't believe luck had anything to do with it. You must have worked your ass off."

She didn't reply, but she couldn't hide her smile. "What about you? How did you get into beer? You mentioned the pub belongs to your dad?"

"The bar was originally my grandfather's. He bought it in the 1960s. But you couldn't distill and distribute alcoholic beverages in Queens until 2007, so my father was into home brewing. And yes, he sold some of that from the house, but don't tell anyone. I got involved when I was a kid, a few years after my mom died. Brewing beer became a thing for me and my dad to do together."

"I'm sorry about your mom, but that's very sweet."

"It was good. It still is. I got more into the chemistry of it all, but he understood beer on an intuitive level. He still does. We work well together."

"So the whole family takes part?"

"Not all of us. A couple of years ago Ruby got a job as an assistant coach for the Indiana Fever women's basketball team. But the rest of us do. You've met Emmy. She works at the bar part-time. There's also Amber and Jade."

"Nice. How come you're not Silver or, I don't know, Sterling?"

"Now, that's where luck really does play a part. My sisters got to name me, and they were in love with Cameron Crowe movies. It was a close call, though. They almost named me Lloyd Dobler."

That made her laugh. How prescient were his sisters? Cameron didn't look like John Cusack in *Say Anything...*, but he possessed that same sincerity that made every girl who'd ever watched the movie fall in love with his character. "It wouldn't have been terrible to be named Lloyd."

"Yes, it would have. I already got enough grief for not being into sports like my sisters, all of whom are older and incredibly coordinated. I didn't need a weirder name than I already have."

"Cam is very butch," she said. "Like something from a car."

He flexed his arm, showing off a good-sized bulge. "That's me, all right. I wear only muscle shirts to work, even when it's ten below outside."

Laughing again, Molly was surprised to find they were both finished with their meals. Which meant she'd get to drag him to her apartment and ravish him until neither of them could move.

He raised his hand to signal the waitress, and that was when it hit her. She couldn't have sex with Cameron Crawford.

It would ruin *everything.*

3

LETTING MOLLY PAY the bill wasn't easy. He'd been raised by fiercely independent women, strong in all kinds of ways and highly opinionated. But in the back of his mind, he heard his father's voice telling him that there was nothing wrong with a little chivalry.

"Are you sure?" he asked before the waitress returned. "You had to do the scary part, so I should pay."

"Are you saying that every time you've asked a woman out, she's footed the bill?"

He grinned. "You're too clever for your own good. You could have made out like a bandit."

Molly shook her head. "You'll notice we didn't go to your favorite restaurant. Besides, I don't think the rules are so set anymore. Not like they used to be."

The waitress took the bill folder and his last chance to pay. At least for this meal. "Tell you what," he said. "Why don't I get the cab?"

Molly's lips parted and she blinked. "Um…"

"Oh. Damn. Sorry. I didn't mean… That was presumptuous, but not intentional. The cab could just be for you. Even if you live in Connecticut, I don't mind." He folded his napkin again, this time putting it on top of his plate instead of on the table. But he had to look at her eventually. When he did, she was smiling. Kind of. Not that big infectious grin he'd seen earlier, but something tighter.

"It's okay. I was thinking about inviting you over for coffee, but I live all the way in Bensonhurst, and I have a terrible apartment and no milk, in case you like milk. In your coffee."

He congratulated himself on turning what had been a relaxed and easy conversation into an awkward mess. "I don't take milk in my coffee, thanks, so we're good. So, Bensonhurst, huh? I haven't been to Little Italy, but I have gone to Chinatown. Do you live near there?"

She nodded, but he was reasonably sure she was still troubled by his assumption. "I have cookies, too. They're just packaged, nothing fancy."

Maybe not that troubled. "I'm not fancy, either. You ready to go?"

She led him through the restaurant as he tried to figure out his next move. He wanted to go to her place. But he'd misconstrued what he'd thought had been a solid green light. Coffee could mean coffee or it could mean sex. He didn't think cookies meant anything but cookies. The only thing to do was let things play out. By the time they got to her place, he'd know what to do.

At almost nine, the August heat was still oppressive. The humid air settled over him like a wet dishrag. There were so many people on the street who looked as if they were partially melted. But not Molly.

It had to be starch that kept her blouse from wilting. He'd never given starch a thought, outside of its chemical properties, but now he wanted to touch her shirt, see if it felt stiff or soft.

Instead, he stepped off the curb and threw his arm up.

He wasn't the only one. Despite the subway station nearby, people wanted cabs, preferably with air-conditioning.

A brush of fingers on his bare arm startled him. He leaned toward her so he could hear her against all the traffic noise.

"Sorry," she said.

He dropped his arm. "Oh—"

"No, not like that. I was going to say something, but I lost the thread. It'll come back to me."

"Sure. Okay."

She smiled. Then she lifted her arm as she turned her attention to the stream of traffic. Not five seconds later, a yellow taxi stopped.

Inside, the cab smelled fresh and felt cool. Molly gave the driver her address, and they both settled in the back, close but not touching.

"I noticed you do a lot of teaching," he said, hoping to recapture the mood from dinner. "Have you ever done that on a wine-tasting cruise?"

Her short laugh was answer enough. "What made you think of that?"

"I saw a commercial. Seven days to Paris and Normandy. It showed a table full of guests with five or six glasses of wine in front of them. It sounded great…until I thought of rough seas."

Molly coughed and laughed at the same time, and he thought she might even be choking. All he could do was pat her back until she held up her hand to stop him. She took a couple of deep, clear breaths before she sat back and dabbed at her eyes with a tissue.

"That was horrible," she said.

"I have no excuse. It was wine related, and my mind just went there, and I can't do anything but apologize."

"I don't think one apology is nearly enough." She shivered. "God, what a picture."

But instead of telling the cabbie to pull over so she could shove him out the door, she giggled. That same light-as-air laugh that he'd heard in the restaurant. For his next trick, he hoped to inspire another wide grin.

"I thought this would be the easiest date in the history of dates," she said.

"Me, too."

"In some ways, it has been." She was staring intently at him. The humor of a minute ago had been replaced with a hint of confusion that Cam didn't understand.

"And not just because of our jobs. Okay, some of it is because of our similar careers, but there was—"

"A connection."

"Yeah."

He'd moved closer to her when she was coughing. His thigh pressed against hers, the top of his arm touched her shoulder. Her eyes widened as he leaned in to press his lips against hers.

She gasped.

He didn't move or breathe.

Until she made it a kiss.

MOLLY INHALED THE SCENT of toasty-rich caramel malt layered with a hint of citrus and spice as she brushed her lips against Cam's. With her eyes closed it was easy to concentrate on the aromas as they spread across the length of her soft palate. But it would take more than scent to reveal the man underneath. At least the air-conditioning wasn't so loud that it blocked the sound of his breath, the click of his swallow.

He pressed forward, opening her mouth, eager for more,

but her hand on his jaw slowed him down long enough for her to run the tip of her tongue across his bottom lip.

She'd studied his mouth in the restaurant. Not in a creepy way, but that plump bottom lip of his was very enticing. He tasted lightly sweet.

He moaned when she slid her tongue past his teeth to where the echo of hops and grains was strongest, but when he pressed back, her train of thought snapped and all she could do was surrender to the far more primal thrust and parry.

This was exactly what she'd hoped for. To find a man to turn off her brain, let her forget the mountain of work that waited on the other side of her front door, the pressure to find time, any kind of time, to sleep without her to-do list jolting her awake.

The way he kissed her, firm and hungry and sure, promised a fantastic vacation of a night, the kind she would remember for weeks when she needed a coma-inducing orgasm after a stressful day.

His hand, large and warm, roamed down her back as he pulled away from the kiss, only to tilt his head to the right, finding an angle that let him pull her body tight against his chest.

The cab's sharp turn parted them too soon.

"You okay?"

Cameron had whispered the words as he stared without blinking. His breathing had morphed into rapid panting, as if he'd run a great distance. She liked knowing that she'd done that to him.

"Good."

She closed her eyes seconds before he kissed her again. They were both leaning now, and in this position she felt smaller. She was normally an expert at making herself disappear in uncomfortable situations, but this was entirely different. Cam was tall. Six-two? Six-three? With his broad chest pressing against her front and his big hands on her back, she felt petite. And petite felt safe. At least with Cameron.

She couldn't hold back a whimper when he stopped, but instead of pulling away his lips went to the sensitive spot behind her ear. He nibbled at her skin, giving her goose bumps, and when he took her earlobe between his teeth, she trembled.

"We need to give the driver a very big tip," she said, her voice high and airy and not like her at all.

"I'll double it if she slows down." He continued kissing her, prompting more whimpers and breathy moans from her, louder now.

Loud enough, evidently.

The taxi decelerated as Molly's heart sped up.

Even if they slowed to a crawl, they were going to get to her place eventually. Tonight could be perfect. Seriously perfect. She even had a bottle of Pinot chilling in the fridge and a new box of condoms in the bathroom cabinet.

God. His hand. His left hand. It wasn't on her back anymore. It was on her breast. Not under her blouse or bra, just resting on top. Way more casual than his rush back to her lips.

For a few seconds, the thrill of the kiss sidetracked her, but then they went over a bump and her hard, sensitive nipple felt the pressure of his hand.

Still. His hand was still. Not squeezing, not doing much of anything. Needing more, she arched her torso.

"There we go," he whispered. "That's what I was waiting for."

"Why?" she asked, seconds before he stole her ability to speak. Not just with his mouth, but the way he touched her. A slow squeeze followed by just his palm circling the tip of her nipple.

The goose bumps came back. Shivers arrived with his low groan.

She caught a peek of orange sky as they stopped, but it was a red light, not home base.

Picturing him in her minuscule apartment made her remember the dress that was hanging in her closet, still covered in plastic. She'd spent too much money on it, even though it was secondhand. But it was for a very special occasion, and as much as Cameron's kisses had reminded her how much she wanted to have mind-boggling sex with him, it was much more important to her to have him escort her to the awards banquet.

But how could she stop this runaway train of sexual exploration? It would be horrible to put the brakes on now.

It wasn't that she felt obligated to have sex with him, even when they were both this aroused. She wanted him. He wanted her. Ever since the first touch of his lips, her body had been giving her an enthusiastic green light. On the other hand... As the cab inched into traffic, Molly pulled back. Not away, not like that, but enough.

"What's wrong?" Cam asked.

"Nothing."

His eyes narrowed. "Uh..."

"I mean, it's something. But nothing's technically wrong."

His left hand dropped away as he sat up, helping her up as he did so. Which was just more proof that he'd be the most perfect date ever for one of the most important nights of her life. Since her neighbor Eddie had moved to Ohio, she didn't have anyone she could count on to be her plus-one.

"Molly?"

When she met Cam's gaze, her uncertainty grew. They

were just two blocks away from her place now, and dammit, she wasn't sure.

She wanted to be sure.

Especially because he'd made it very clear he had one goal in mind, and if they both went upstairs, he'd get his wish and walk away. And while she'd be left sexually satisfied, she would lose a golden opportunity. Getting the award, making the speech, being in the company of so many people she admired terrified her.

Her only option was to move the goal line.

Fully aware that she was being manipulative and selfish, she plunged ahead. "I'm sorry. So, so sorry. I know my timing is terrible, but please, could I have a rain check?"

His shocked expression almost convinced her to change her mind.

"I have to admit I was not expecting that," he said. "Did I get my signals crossed?"

"No. Everything you did was great. Perfect. I didn't know until just now that I wasn't sure. About the rest of it. About moving so fast. This has been a fantastic night, but…"

"You need to be certain."

She nodded.

He looked at her with his dark eyes. "Okay. Rain check it is."

Her sigh didn't ease her guilt, but it did help her relax enough to grab her purse. "I'll call you," she said, just as they turned onto her block. "Soon. Very soon. I hope you'll want to see me again."

Cam leaned over and kissed her. Lightly. On the lips, and then on her cheek. "I had a great time," he said. "Almost all the way to the end."

She winced, even though he was teasing. "Thank you." She found his hand and squeezed it before she opened her purse to pull out her wallet. "I'm sorry about the coffee."

"There's nothing to apologize for," he said, stopping her from getting money out. "Can you wait for me?" he asked the cabbie. "Five minutes?"

"I'm on the clock. Take your time."

"You don't need to walk me up," Molly said. "Honestly. I appreciate it, but I'll be fine. I've only got a few steps to go before I'm inside."

Nodding, he got out of the cab and held his hand out to help her. Once they were standing on the sidewalk, she had the urge to ask him up anyway, but she held back. She wanted him to be the perfect ending to her big awards night. Then, when they said their goodbyes, she'd have no regrets at all.

THE RIDE BACK to Manhattan was as surreal as it was uncomfortable. Cam had been completely blindsided by Molly's request. The conversation had been stellar. She was amazing to touch, to kiss, and the way she'd kissed him back—

Dammit, there'd been chemistry between them.

Not *the forever* kind. But it had been easy and sexy. Naturally, he'd pictured them in bed together. Halfway to her place, he'd been calculating how early they'd have to get up to have morning sex.

And then…ice water.

At least the physical discomfort had eased up. Not totally. That wouldn't happen until he got back to his place and did some manual labor. But at least his balls weren't blue anymore.

Even though he'd moved to the side of the bench seat, he knew the cabbie was still sneaking glimpses at him. A woman behind the wheel was a rarity in New York. He'd have liked to ask her opinion about what had happened, but that would be admitting he'd been making out in the backseat like a teenage horndog. Of course, she knew that.

No way she couldn't, but pretending that it hadn't happened was the best way to handle things like this.

Besides, Cam was pretty certain Molly had meant what she'd said. That she would call him, and they'd have another go, and she'd have quelled her doubts. Huh. She'd probably gone directly to the internet to check out his story. She'd met Emmy, but when it came down to taking a man into her bed, she probably wanted to be completely confident he wasn't a bastard.

He'd checked her out. Why wouldn't she do the same?

Right. It wasn't complicated, and it wasn't about him. Maybe he should have insisted on paying the dinner tab.

No. She'd been very clear, and his sisters had taught him to listen to things like that. Ignoring the express wishes of a lady, even if he thought he knew better, was dismissive and a dick move.

That she'd postponed things meant nothing. Sex tonight hadn't been cut in stone. The next move was hers. He hoped she'd call. If she didn't? No need to go there. He hadn't even gotten back to the city yet. He'd give it a few days. She'd call.

She would.

4

FOUR A.M. As he stared at the ceiling, thoughts of Molly and what they could have been doing kept Cam up, pissed that he couldn't turn off his brain.

Since the date had ended earlier than he'd expected, he'd gone down to the bar to help out after his shower. The plan had been to get some relief then hit the sack, but that hadn't worked out, either.

Sunday through Thursday, they were open till two. As soon as their last customer left, Cam had helped the Sunday night crew clean everything. He'd made an excellent favor swap with Solomon, their senior bartender. Solomon now owed him a weekend night off for scrubbing the floors in the kitchen and subbing in behind the bar. The physical exercise and focus had been a good distraction from thinking about Molly. Unfortunately, the distraction had stopped working as soon as he had.

He'd tried to convince himself he was tired enough to sleep. After lying in bed as the minutes marched on, he went for one more round with his right hand. It didn't take long to get hard, not when he could picture her so clearly. Shit, he could still practically feel her breast under his palm.

If this didn't do the trick, he'd get out his notebook and work some calculus problems. Those had always put him to sleep.

MOLLY SQUIRMED IN her bed, unable to find a comfortable position. She wouldn't look at the clock. Not again. Every time she did, she was compelled to figure out how many hours she had until her alarm went off if she immediately fell asleep.

The last reading had been at two-fifteen. Her alarm would go off at five-thirty.

All because she was the most horrible person in all of New York. And New Jersey, and probably Connecticut and, what the hell, Rhode Island, too.

The look on Cameron's face when she'd pulled the emergency cord. She might as well have slapped him across the face. What she'd actually done was probably worse for a guy.

She'd been having this internal debate since she'd walked into her apartment and turned on her computer. She'd gone straight to The Four Sisters Brewpub's website. It was an impressive site with lots of history about the place, including how many blue ribbons Cameron's beer had won in the past. But none in the past five years.

They'd barely scratched the surface of each other's lives. She had questions. Far too many for a brief encounter of the sexual kind. Where had he gone to school? What did he do when he wasn't crafting beers, or was he like her, obsessed and never truly away from his career?

The world of wine was very competitive. Very few made any kind of splash at all, and barely a trickle became internationally noted.

She wished Phillip and Simone had planned on coming to New York for Friday's ceremony. But it was understandable that they couldn't just drop everything for one banquet. Bordeaux to New York was a major trip, and they were so busy with the vineyard and the business. Simone had mentioned a possible visit in the fall, so that was something to look forward to.

In the meantime, if Molly had Cam on her arm, no one would wonder where her parents were. Of course, Phillip and Simone weren't her real parents; she'd known them for only twelve years. But they'd brought her into their incredible home, into their lives. It had been a rebirth, the only one that mattered to her.

She'd have liked to introduce them to Cameron. He'd have gotten on well with Phillip especially. Phillip enjoyed a cold beer from time to time, although you would never guess it. But he'd have liked that Cameron was the brains behind his brews.

And now here Molly was, unable to sleep, her mind still chock-full of Cameron. Which wasn't wise. She barely knew him, and best-case scenario, she'd be with him from Friday evening through Saturday morning. If she was very lucky, maybe they'd have breakfast together, but that thought, that hope, was already crossing a line.

She'd lived on fantasies most of her life. Only one had ever come true. Phillip and Simone hadn't actually adopted her, but that was okay. Just the odds of finding an amazing foster family as a teenager were off the charts.

Her thoughts veered back to the most vivid of tonight's fantasies. Cameron, taking off her clothes. Slowly. Kissing all the places he uncovered. Calling her beautiful, even though she knew she wasn't quite. It was easy to picture him without his shirt. Not so easy to imagine what was under his jeans. At least in the front. She'd already gotten a great look at his butt with the way the denim hugged him.

He did have big hands, so… That didn't necessarily

mean he was well-endowed, but for now, she'd go with it. What the heck, right? In for a penny. Having already used her vibrator once, she let her fingers do the work this time. Once they were underneath her panties, she knew exactly what to do. Her imagination was vivid and well practiced. He'd be on this very bed, the covers tossed aside. His kisses were easy to recall in perfect detail. From there, she could extrapolate what his lips would feel like on her nipples. How he'd lick his way down until he reached her button.

She winced at the word, the old word that she'd learned from the other kids. When they'd whispered after lights-out. *The button*. It had taken her years to figure out what they meant. She'd thought it was a real button.

She'd learned, of course, that it was her clitoris. But some habits were harder to break than others, and dammit, she didn't want to think about anything but Cameron and how he'd know just what she liked. How he'd go slowly until she couldn't stand it, and how he would care more about making her happy than just taking for himself. Hey, it was her fantasy, so she didn't care that men like that didn't exist in real life.

She'd call him on Tuesday. Give him enough time to rent a tuxedo, if he didn't own one. Would he be insulted if she offered to pay for the rental?

Pulling her hand out of her pants, she gave up. She was never going to get to sleep if she didn't stop projecting wildly about a man she barely knew.

All she had was a feeling.

Cameron Crawford would come through for her. For one perfect night. Was that too much to hope for?

Sighing, she avoided answering her own question and started counting the seconds, determined to get to five hundred or fall asleep trying.

She reached eight hundred and nine.

"I'M GONNA CALL HER." It was Tuesday afternoon and Emmy was prepping condiments while Cameron worked at the small table in the corner of the bar's kitchen. "As a friend," he said. "Just, you know, make sure she's okay."

Emmy was quiet for so long, Cam looked up. She wasn't looking at him. In fact, she was standing at the sink washing limes, but there was no doubt she was judging him.

"I'm not going to make a big deal out of it. Besides, I'll hear it in her voice if she doesn't want to talk to me." Hell, she probably wouldn't even answer. Stupid caller ID. There weren't any surprises left in life.

"You sure that's a good idea?"

He glanced down at his newest recipe for a cream ale. Although he hadn't gotten nearly enough sleep last night, at least he'd come up with what he thought was a viable design for a unique brew. But his mind wasn't on the new ale. It was stuck on all the things he wished he'd said to Molly.

What the hell? Last time he'd checked, he wasn't a teenage girl.

Closing his eyes, he let his chin drop to his chest. "I should go back to bed. Fifteen minutes is all I need. I read an article. Fifteen, twenty minutes is supposed to leave me refreshed but not groggy." He looked at his sister again. "It sounds like torture. Maybe that's why it works. I'll end up so pissed off that I couldn't enjoy my nap, it'll knock that groggy shit right out."

Emmy laughed. Turned off the water. "What's gotten into you? You must have really liked Molly, because you never mention women you go out with. Even the ones that keep you out all night."

He wasn't about to tell Emmy how the date had actually ended. Way too much information, and just…no. "We didn't really finish our conversation, that's all. She was nice. Interesting."

"Your conversation. Uh-huh."

"I'm tired. Leave me alone. Actually, talk to Jade. She's trying to set me up with someone from her gym. I told her about the trading cards, but I could tell she's got something cooking."

"Fine. I'll talk to her. Just do me a favor. Don't call Molly. You sound pathetic."

"Thanks a lot." He was supposed to finish writing this damn recipe, then go help pitch the yeast into the wort. Eric was running the floor in back, and the crew would do just fine without him, but an extra hand was never turned away. They'd all helped him with his small-brew experiments. Yeah, that was part of what they got paid to do, but it never felt like that, not in the brewery or the bar. You made the payroll, you became part of The Four Sisters family.

"Don't forget to talk to Jade."

"Yes, sir." Emmy turned back to her prepping, and Cam left the kitchen. Left the bar. Only to go upstairs to his apartment.

His dad had had this addition built. There'd been plenty of times that a place to crash had been a blessing, and Cam was sure everyone would be relieved when he went back to Syracuse. Fridays and Saturdays the bar was open until four in the morning. A lot of people had crashed in the bed upstairs.

It wasn't even that noisy. The contractor had previously worked on sound booths and editing facilities, and he'd made sure not much noise bled upstairs. Nothing they could do about the vibrations, but Cam was used to the pulse of the jukebox.

Halfway up, his cell phone rang, and when he saw it was Molly, he hurried up the rest of the stairs. He didn't answer until he was inside the apartment with the door shut behind him.

"Hi. It's Molly."

"I know. How are you?"

"I'm fine. Good. I mean, I'm completely stuck on this column I'm writing, but other than that, everything's fine."

"I'm glad. Not about being stuck. About…" He took a deep breath and let it out slowly. He could do better. "I was impressed when I saw that you blocked out time on your calendar for writing and stuff."

"I just wanted people to know that I have office hours. That it would be better not to call when I was working."

"Do they anyway?"

She laughed. "All the time."

"It was worth a try, though, huh?"

"Yeah."

He could hear the smile in her voice.

"I'm still awfully sorry for how I left things," she said, using her serious voice again. "It wasn't very nice of me."

"It's okay. It really is. Especially now that you've called back."

"Right. About that rain check."

"Say when."

She was silent for several beats—enough time for him to realize he'd jumped the gun again. Why couldn't he wait for the punch line with her?

"Well, actually, I was thinking about Friday night. Except there's a catch."

He sat down on the one really comfortable chair in the apartment. The place wasn't big. A round table and chairs next to a tiny kitchen that wasn't much more than a cooktop, a dorm fridge, a microwave and a sink. There was also a bathroom—shower only, no tub—and a queen-size bed. The good chair wasn't huge, just comfortable. "I'm listening," he said, wondering what the catch could possibly be.

"There's a thing I need to go to. A banquet, actually. It's a wine thing, so there'll be fantastic drinks and food. But it's formal, so yeah, a tux would help, and there'll be some speeches, so that won't be fun. Except when I say there'll be great wine, I mean it. All the top vineyards send their best stuff."

"A banquet?"

"Yeah. For the industry. Wine writers. It's an international association, and people come from all over to attend. I don't think you'll be too bored. There'll be nice people at our table. Really nice people. Like Donna. My editor. She's the editor in chief of the magazine, and she's hilarious. She's completely New York and doesn't give a damn who likes her or not, so she never holds back. I know she'd like you, too."

Cam should stop her. He'd already decided to go. Hell, if she'd asked him to accompany her to the moon, he'd have rented an astronaut suit. A tuxedo was nothing.

"It sounds great and the tux isn't a problem. You just tell me what time and where to show up."

"Really?'

He grinned and stretched out in his chair, putting his free hand behind his head. "Really. So, is this a mandatory work thing, or is this something you like doing?"

"I'm always amazed I get to go, although they usually charge for a place at the table."

"What's unusual about this time?"

She cleared her throat, although it was muted, as if she'd moved the phone away from her mouth. "Well, I'm getting an award."

"No kidding? What for?"

"Emerging wine writer of the year." He could picture her so easily, the way she'd look down, then back up at him through her lashes.

Now he was even more pleased that he'd said yes. "That's very impressive. I imagine there was a lot of competition for that award. I'm going to have to read all of your columns now. I only sampled a few, but they were excellent. Huh. It'll be like going to the Oscars with Jennifer Lawrence."

She laughed. "It's so not. Not by a mile."

"You can have your fantasies and I'll have mine. At the very least, I'll be with the prettiest woman there."

"You make me blush. But I'll give you a hint. You don't have to do that."

"What?"

"Compliment me so lavishly."

He shook his head. "I'm not. I mean what I say."

"Right."

"Next time you see Emmy, you ask her what I'm like. I'm not prone to exaggeration. Honest to a fault, and I mean that literally. I say too much, too often. Probably because I had four older sisters to compete with. But how come you know you've won? Aren't these things supposed to be a surprise?"

"Not really. Some of the recipients live far away, so they let them know in advance."

"I wish they'd do that in beer competitions, but I suppose they can't. I hate the nerves that come before they announce the winners."

"I really want to talk to you about beer," she said. "I want to know about the brewing processes and the subculture and what the politics are like."

It was clear she meant it, and he loved that she was interested, although it was such a huge topic that he had no idea where to start. "But I can't. Not right now. I've got a meeting in a few minutes. I sort of planned it this way. I wanted an excuse to end the conversation quickly in case you said no."

"You could have made something up," he said, wishing she didn't have a meeting.

"I'm honest to a fault, too. Although not as a statement or a philosophy. I'm just a lousy liar."

"Another reason to look forward to Friday night."

She sighed, and he wanted to kiss her. "Thank you. I'll be in touch."

"Great." After the call ended, he thought about what Emmy had said and wondered what it was about Molly that had him so wound up. Probably the fact that she didn't want a relationship. He'd hated those family setups. The only thing he was looking for while he was in Queens was a good time. No strings, no complications. Luckily, that appeared to be all that Molly wanted, as well.

5

IT WAS CAMERON. On her cell. Molly straightened her hair and mashed her lips together to spread her berry lip balm as if he could see her on Skype. After taking a couple of full breaths, the way she did before each broadcast, she answered the call. "Hello?"

"You're working. I don't want to bother you. But then I figured if you were too busy, you'd let it go to voice mail. Are you too busy?"

"Nope." And she'd said she didn't lie well. "What's up?"

"I need your opinion."

Molly heard some muffled noises, nothing she could really interpret, then her phone beeped. She pulled it away from her ear to see who it was, only to discover it was Cam. She clicked on his message and a picture started to load.

Hers wasn't one of the latest smartphones on the market, but it was decent enough to display a clear photo. Her grin grew as she realized he'd sent her a selfie—and not a good one because of the flash flaring in the mirror. She could barely make out Cam in a black tuxedo.

A faint "Hey" made her click on the speaker. "Molly! Did I lose you?"

"No, I'm here," she said. "And I've turned on the speaker. So, I assume you're picking out your tux."

"No, I'm having lunch at Prune. This is how I always dress."

"Ha. I like a man with a subtle sense of humor. I can't actually see what the tux looks like. Is there someone in the shop who could get a better shot of you?"

"Yeah, I think so. The guy running the place probably wouldn't mind. Hold on. I only put on the jacket."

The sounds that followed painted another picture entirely. First his phone clunked on something hard, and then there was the unmistakable swoosh of fabric on fabric. Was he taking off his own clothes to try on the tux pants? Or had he called her wearing no pants at all?

"Okay," he said, and his voice got louder. "Let's go find a photographer."

"I can't believe you're going to all this trouble."

"This is important," he said. "I'm going with one of the honorees. She's the emerging wine writer of the year. The event's very classy. And so is she."

Now she was grinning like a lunatic. She should get up, lock her door. Two students had appointments starting about five minutes ago. Not at the same time. Back-to-back. But Tanya was late, so her loss. By the time Molly did turn the lock, there was another voice coming from her Android. He had a pretty thick accent. Spanish, she thought, although there was noise filtering in from the street.

Soon enough, her phone beeped again. This time she could clearly make out the tux and Cam. He looked gorgeous. The lapels on his tux were wide enough to fly him cross-country, but everything else was perfect.

"Yes?" he asked. "No?"

"Not sure about the lapels," she told him, hoping there was an alternative.

"Okay. Stay right there. I'll be right back."

She wished she could see it all. Be there while he tried things on. But the fact that he was going to so much effort for her? All her doubts about inviting him had left the building and she no longer felt even a smidgen of guilt. He *was* the perfect escort, and she couldn't wait for Friday. Only two more days to go.

She'd tried to convince him to meet her at the hotel, but he'd insisted on picking her up at her apartment.

"You there?" He was yelling again.

"Yes!"

"Hold on."

The beep came and this time he'd posed like a movie star, turned slightly to the right, with his eyes looking directly into the camera. It took a few seconds for her to remember to check out the suit.

"Much better," she said. "You look wonderful. Very handsome."

"Yeah?" he asked, sounding pleased.

"Yeah."

"I'll take it," he said. Then a moment later, "Molly? Thank you. I'm glad I called. Talk to you later, okay?"

She nodded. "More than okay."

When her first student knocked, she was still holding her phone. Smiling.

IT SHOULD HAVE BEEN dark by the time Cam arrived at Molly's apartment. It felt weird to be decked out in his rented tux when it was still daylight as he walked from the cab to the entrance of the five-story building. There wasn't a doorman, just an intercom. He pressed number 403 and she buzzed him in.

The lobby was nothing flashy, but it was clean, which was something in this part of New York. As the elevator rose, it occurred to him that he was nervous again. Why she brought out the teenager in him, he wasn't sure. She wasn't that much younger than he was. Jesus, he'd been dating for eighteen years. Not continuously. He'd had girlfriends, but the only one who had lasted had been Robin. They'd been together three years after meeting at MIT. Still, even fifteen years of dating seemed like a lot.

But right now Molly was the only person on his radar. It might be all about the sex, but he was also looking forward to spending time with her again.

Finally, the elevator made it to the fourth floor, and it was only a few steps to her door. He knocked, glad to see she had a peephole. There was some unpleasantly aggressive noise coming from an apartment down the hall.

Molly opened the door and he forgot all about the neighbors. "You look beautiful."

She'd been worrying her lower lip, but at his words, she gave him a spectacular smile. "Thank you. I put this on and immediately hated it. I've changed four times, but I don't have anything else nearly as nice. If you'd looked at me funny, I probably would have broken down in tears."

He didn't wait for an invitation. He just walked right in, took her hand and had her twirl around in her body-hugging white dress. It was strapless and deeply sexy. He'd thought of her as delicate, but that didn't describe her now. Not with her thick hair pulled up, baring her long, pale neck, her lips full and pink, and the way the dress skimmed over her body like his hands ached to do. "So unnecessary," he said. "The worry, I mean. You really look stunning."

She blinked fast. Waved her hands in front of her eyes. "Don't you dare make me cry. I went to Macy's and had the manager of the cosmetics department put all this on."

Well, there went his plans to kiss her until they both

couldn't breathe. "All this? What, mascara? Pink lipstick? You're too pretty to cover your face with makeup."

She sighed. "You couldn't have given me a better compliment."

He didn't understand her reaction, but he wasn't going to argue. "You ready? I'm not sure about the traffic from here."

"I'll get my bag."

While she went to her bedside table, he glanced around the apartment. It was about half the size of his. Everything was in one room, except for the bathroom. Which must have just been a toilet and sink, because the bathtub was in what would have been called a kitchen, if someone felt generous. She could easily lean out from behind the circular shower curtain to pour herself a cup of coffee. The microwave was too small for a Hungry-Man dinner. The bed was going to be a tight fit later that night, and, weirdly, there were what looked like built-in storage cupboards above the headboard.

In addition, there was a dresser, a mirror, two chairs, a small table covered with books, a laptop and a stack of magazines. That was it. But she'd definitely made it her own. There were wine charts on the wall, maps of the different vineyards in France, Napa Valley and Italy, and a large whiteboard hanging near the bathroom. It had a more detailed schedule written on it, along with a to-do list. The other big item was a wine-cooler fridge, and that was plugged in next to the bed instead of the eating area. Ah, and how had he missed the wine rack on top of the dorm-sized refrigerator?

"I'm all set," she said, holding a tiny red purse. "But first, may I say you look amazingly handsome in that tuxedo. I can't thank you enough for being such a good sport about this."

"Good sport, nothing. I'm looking forward to it. Especially now that I'm going to make every guy in the place jealous."

She shook her head, leading his gaze to the stretch of bare skin from her chin to the tops of her breasts. The evening couldn't go fast enough for him.

"Let's go. I've got a thing about being on time."

He bent at the waist and held out his hand. "I'm at your service."

"Oh, you're going to be a big hit with all the ladies tonight."

He appreciated the compliment, but the only one he cared about impressing was her.

GETTING INTO THE TAXI in her dress wasn't easy. She'd thought that perhaps Simone and Phillip would have sent a car, but she hadn't heard a word from them. Which was fine. She was sure they'd surprise her with something special to mark the occasion, and that whatever it was would be perfect.

People from her building were standing on the stoop, staring at Cameron, mostly, but that wasn't an issue. She barely knew any of her neighbors. Mrs. Waverley lived next door in 401, and they exchanged favors from time to time. Accepting a package, getting mail. One Christmas, she'd given Molly a loaf of her special-recipe banana bread.

Molly arranged her dress so it wouldn't wrinkle too badly and tried to get comfortable, pleased that Cameron had held the cab, with the meter running, because the airconditioning felt great. It would have sucked to arrive at the hotel drenched in sweat.

The ride was going to cost a fortune, though. She had enough room on her credit card to cover a number of catastrophes, everything from having to spend the night at the hotel to emergency clothing replacements. But she had the feeling Cam wouldn't let her pay even half.

While he spoke to the driver, her discomfort reared its head again. Excited as she was to be given the award, she dreaded these social gatherings. They were never easy for her no matter what the circumstance. She opened her purse, which was just big enough to hold her folded notes, lipstick, key and money.

"All right?" Cam asked as he touched the back of her hand.

"Nervous. But I've got my speech in my purse."

"Ah, I wondered if you'd have to give one."

"I don't mind. It's mostly thank-you stuff. The magazine took a chance with me. One that's made a big difference in my life. The wine world is big on accolades and prizes. I imagine it's the same thing with beer."

He nodded slowly, as if she'd said something he needed to consider. "Especially with craft beers. Yeah. But here's something that's been bothering me since you opened the door. That lipstick you're wearing—is it difficult to put on?"

"Not particularly."

"So it wouldn't ruin anything if I kissed you? A lot? Perhaps all the way to the banquet?"

Molly smiled, feeling a bit of that giddiness he seemed to inspire, not sure if he was teasing or not. "I might need to breathe from time to time. Oh, and I wanted to fill you in on who's going to be at our table—"

"Other than that?" he asked, his mouth so close, the scent of wintergreen made her want to taste him.

"Other than that, I don't see any problem at—"

He stole the last word, but she didn't mind. She'd wanted to kiss him, too, and would have if she hadn't been so focused on getting out the door. Since their date, they'd spoken on the phone four times, and those conversations had fueled her libido way more than any of the men she'd actually been with.

Cam was being so careful, it made her heart swell. His palm was on the nape of her neck, his other hand on her waist, touching her lightly, as if she were made of spun glass.

"I've been thinking about kissing you since Sunday's taxi ride," he whispered, nuzzling her ear.

His lips moved down her neck, then lower still, to just above her bodice. His breath was warm and shivery, and she touched the back of his head to keep him right there, but when the taxi stopped for a red light, she let him go.

He stopped what he was doing, but not for long. He revisited the sensitive skin on her neck. After several kisses, he licked the shell of her ear. "I hope this doesn't become a problem. It could be embarrassing if I have to share a cab with someone who isn't you."

Her brain had stopped working for a while, but now she had to wonder if he was being literal about his reaction to her. He had just shifted around a bit.

He pulled away from her, enough to look into her eyes. "Okay, I need to cool down. Tell me about tonight."

It took her a moment to gather her wits and realize that her racing heartbeat wasn't entirely his fault. "I can't decide if tonight is scarier than taking the master-sommelier exams or not."

"Different kind of scary, I imagine," he said, his breathing uneven.

"If I hadn't passed, only a few people would have been disappointed in me. Tonight, all the bigwigs from the magazine are going to be there, and a lot of other columnists and bloggers and experts from every facet of the business.

I should have called in sick. Donna could have thanked everyone for me."

"Donna? Editor in chief, right? The woman I need to thank profusely for introducing you to the trading cards?"

Her jaw dropped. She'd forgotten she'd mentioned Donna to him. It was crazy how great he was. It was probably a good thing she wouldn't be seeing him again after tonight because he really was distracting.

She simply had to kiss him again, and this time she made sure he wasn't so careful. When she finally had to cry uncle in order to get her breath back, his hair was messed up and his eyes looked glazed.

"Well, damn," he said. "How long is this banquet supposed to last?"

"It'll probably go pretty late, but don't fret. We won't stay till the bitter end because I have a class tomorrow morning. Which is a shame because you'd be hard-pressed to find a better assortment of wine in Manhattan. I mean, the whole event is about honoring writers, and the vintners want the free press."

"Good to know," he said. "Uh, if you're going to tell me who's who, you'd better talk fast because we're a block from the hotel."

She'd been nervous all day, but that was child's play compared to what she felt now. "You know what? You'll figure it out. Oh, God, we're here. It's actually happening."

After one last scorching kiss, he paid the fare while she panicked. Before she walked into the ballroom, she needed to get it together. For God's sake, the world wasn't going to end if she messed up. It would be fine. Cameron would help fill any awkward gaps. That was the whole point of him.

She jumped when a uniformed bellman opened her door. He must have been sweltering with his fancy jacket buttoned all the way to his neck. She jumped again when

Cameron put his arm around her waist. "I've got you," he said, his voice soft and close.

Behind the bellman, she saw Donna walking toward them, but she wasn't alone.

"Oh, God," Molly said, gripping Cameron's arm. "That's Robert Parker, probably the most influential wine writer in the world. And Benjamin Spencer from *American Wine Writer.* And Donna and her date. They're almost here." Molly looked up into Cameron's gaze. "Do me a favor? Don't let me go, okay? Not until we're at our table."

He nodded, smiled, then bent down and kissed her yet again.

She was so shocked, she forgot to kiss him back. All she could do was hang on. Then she felt his thumb rub against the side of her mouth, and the fingers of his other hand touched the back of her chignon.

He pulled away seconds before the others arrived. Then he winked and whispered, "Now you're ready to knock 'em dead."

"Oh," she said, touching where he'd obviously fixed her smudged lipstick. Too good to be true, maybe, but for tonight, he was perfect.

6

CAMERON HAD BEEN to his share of professional events, but this wine crowd was something else. It was like walking onto a movie set. Everything seemed to sparkle. There were at least twelve tables of eight, with nine wineglasses lined up in front of each place setting, like spokes in a very fancy wheel. A draped exhibition table ran the length of the far wall, displaying bottles of reds and whites. Up front was a smallish stage set with a table of tall, vaguely wine-bottle-shaped statues, a dais and microphone, and a large overhead screen playing a slide show of people, vineyards and bottles of wine.

Cam had taken Molly's arm as they'd walked to the banquet itself. Introductions had been brief, and except for Donna, who reminded him of Penny Marshall, Cam wasn't worried about forgetting any names. He'd been to plenty of events where he was expected to mingle. Few were this fancy, however. Molly's nervousness made more sense now that he understood the atmosphere. This banquet was more Oscars than Oktoberfest.

Molly seemed to be creating quite a stir. He noticed a lot of people looking at her—and not discreetly, either. Once they'd located their table and had accepted a glass of the premeal Champagne on offer, Donna walked up to Cameron and said, "If I'd known you'd look so good in a tux, I wouldn't have given your trading card to Molly."

"I'm grateful you did," he said. "Although I can already tell you'd have been a great date." He put his drink down and turned to her escort. Their introduction had been interrupted earlier, so Cam held out his hand. "Wayne, is it?" he asked, and the man nodded. "Cameron Crawford. Congratulations on your good fortune."

"And to you, as well," Wayne said, smiling happily. "So, you're one of those trading-card guys, are you?"

"Yes. My sister got me involved, and the rest is history. Have you met Molly Grainger? She's here to collect her emerging-wine-writer-of-the-year award."

Molly smiled at Wayne as she pressed herself a little more closely to Cam. It wasn't the most convenient place to chat, huddled next to the table, and with his arm around Molly, Cameron didn't get to drink any more of his Champagne, which was a pity. But he wasn't about to let go of her.

As they mingled, he began to see a pattern. Someone would approach Molly and congratulate her on her award, maybe mention a specific column or her radio show, and after a few short words she would shift the ball to his court, which inevitably led to a discussion that didn't include her at all. Not that she couldn't have joined in. He tried including her the first few times. But she seemed far more relaxed to be listening than participating.

She had all the earmarks of someone with social anxiety, although she hid it well. If he hadn't been paying such close attention, he'd have thought nothing of her behavior. He doubted a single person in their circle would remember that Molly had hardly said a word.

By the time they were asked to take their seats, he'd

learned to identify how nervous she was by the pressure of her body against his. So he asked a lot of questions, mentioned Molly's columns without making her blush too much and generally kept things moving along. He was glad these kinds of situations were easy for him. His talent for small talk was a gift, one he'd used to his advantage in college and on the beer circuit.

He held Molly's chair, then sat down himself. Bending close to her ear, he put his hand on hers and asked her quietly if she was okay.

She turned her palm over so her fingers threaded through his. "Yes, thank you. You have no idea how much I appreciate you being here tonight. I would have been a complete mess on my own. As I'm sure you've guessed, I don't mingle well. Give me a class to teach or a wine to discuss, and I'm good to go, but the small talk…not so much."

"I thought you were great, and no, don't shake your head. You should believe me. After all, I was right about you being the most beautiful woman in the room."

"You're a liar, but a sweet one."

He wanted to kiss her, but that might draw too much attention. Instead, he squeezed her hand and lifted his now-flat drink for a private toast. "To the guest of honor."

She laughed. "I'm really not."

"That's good, too. Less pressure when it's time to make your speech."

"I think you'll be surprised," she said, then took one more sip. "Just don't expect any extemporaneous anecdotes."

"Deal."

The room darkened, and a silver-haired man took the stage. The applause was generous, but Cam wasn't sure if it was because they all knew who he was or because the first round of wineglasses was finally being filled. The master of ceremonies introduced the vintage before he introduced himself. It was a Maison Louis Jadot Savigny-lès-Beaune Clos des Guettes Premier Cru Blanc 2011, to be accompanied by a rabbit, spring vegetable and pistachio terrine. *Très sophistiqué.*

Cam looked at Molly. "What do you think of the pairing?"

"Won't know until I try it." She grinned. "But considering the occasion, I'm reasonably sure you can trust the selections."

He smiled back and sampled the rabbit terrine, then had a sip of wine. Together, they were far more unforgettable than their names. The fun part was watching all the wine nerds swirl, sniff and slurp as they tasted. He saw a lot more raised eyebrows and facial tics than he was used to. At least he wasn't the only amateur at the table. Although Cam could discern some things about the wine that the general populace would miss, he was definitely out of his league in this room full of wine aficionados.

As the evening progressed, the conversation at the table turned more jovial. Wine tended to loosen things up, and he wasn't the only one who was finishing each glass. Admittedly, the portions were small, but they added up.

"You're attending the Long Island Wine Camp this year, aren't you, Molly?"

James Furulya, a master sommelier and consultant, had asked the question. He'd come without a date, and Cam had noticed early on that he was more interested in Molly than the Gérard Bertrand Domaine de Cigalus IGP Something Something.

"Yes," she said. "I'll be there. I'm doing the food-and-wine-pairing event and teaching three classes."

"Fantastic," he said. "Can't wait to see what kinds of wines you choose. I love listening to your radio show."

Molly paused with her fork in midair, then went back to her plate. "Don't tell me you listen to *Wine for Newbies*."

"Not every week," he said with a wry smile. "But often enough."

Cameron disliked him. He was far too old for Molly, and if he thought his comb-over was fooling anyone, he was out of touch. He was also the only one of the six strangers at the table who hadn't introduced himself to Cam.

"I'm flattered. Thank you. I've heard the camp is great fun for everyone. At those prices, it better be, huh?"

"Oh, that's nothing," Comb-Over said. "I once hosted a single-day event in Silicon Valley that charged over five thousand dollars a head."

"What were they serving?" she asked.

Furulya responded. In detail. Then he invited Molly to another wine event taking place in late September. It sounded snooty as hell. The whole time, he never once shifted his gaze away from Molly's.

The only thing that shut him up was the announcement for the next award. It was Molly's category, and amid all the applause when her name was announced, Cam stood up with her, worried and pleased and more nervous than he'd been at any of his own competitions.

She gave Donna a one-shoulder hug and turned back to him. "I'm okay," she said.

"Go get 'em, tiger."

Finally, she smiled like a winner—that great smile he'd seen the first night.

He didn't sit down until she was at the dais and had lowered the mike.

"Thank you very much to the members of the International Wine Writers Association for this incredible honor. I wouldn't be standing here if it weren't for the generosity of my editor, Donna Woppner, and the whole team at *Wine*

Connoisseur. Thank you for giving me all the encourage-
ment and support a newbie could hope for. And a special
thanks to Phillip and Simone Alexander for introducing
me to the world of enology. It's a privilege to be here with
so many legends in the industry."

That was it. Short and sweet, but from the reaction of
her fellows, she appeared to be a big hit. Cam wouldn't
have guessed she'd be so confident on that stage. A hundred questions about her spun in his head, but he'd ask exactly none of them. Tonight was for celebrating.

MOLLY SHOULD HAVE BEEN listening to the closing speech,
but she couldn't stop thinking about the evening and how
different it had been from any of the social engagements
she'd attended in the past. Not because she'd won a prize.
If anything, that should have made things ten times worse.
She'd never done well at large functions, and when she'd
told Cameron that she wasn't comfortable with small talk,
it had been the understatement of the year.

It wasn't as if Cam's presence had miraculously trans-
formed her into a social butterfly. Not at all. Without a
concrete task to perform, she was pretty much hopeless
and most often wound up hiding in the restroom for ages
or drinking too much.

Tonight, Cameron had done all the hard work. He was
wonderful with strangers—charismatic, charming—and
yet he did that great thing where he made everyone else
feel interesting. After a few conversations, she'd come
to anticipate Cameron's questions. They were always in-
sightful and there was no doubt his curiosity was genuine.
The person he was talking to would invariably stand up
straighter and ignore the complimentary Champagne for
the more flattering attention. Cam even knew how to make

a perfect exit. One that reminded them again of whom he was with and how proud of her he was.

All in all, it had been a pretty magical evening. It seemed hard to believe that not only was the event over, but she hadn't even noticed the time flying by. She should have left at least an hour ago. Cam had excused himself for a few minutes, and Donna sidled up to her. "You were great up there," she said. "Like a seasoned pro."

"I practiced," Molly admitted. "A lot."

"Good for you. It paid off." Leaning closer, Donna said, "He is so scrumptious, I can hardly stand it. You can't let him go."

"Come on, Donna. As if I have a choice? You saw his card. He's only here tonight because we never…you know."

"That's not the only reason he's here. No one's that attentive if all they're after is a one-night stand."

Molly shook her head.

"When Eddie was your date, he barely spoke to anyone, including you. Cameron was here for you, not the food and drinks. It's like you've been a couple for years."

"He'd have been that way with anyone. I told you he was great."

Donna narrowed her gaze. "You've got some strange notions, Molly. Seriously strange. Look, go home, have a ball, but don't assume anything. Play it out, see where it goes."

She shook her head. "What's the use? You know I can't afford to get involved like that."

"You and your damn schedule." Donna sighed. "I admire your ambition, hon, but all work and no play—"

"Gives me a huge advantage. Because everyone else is out there dating and flirting and juggling appointments and missing deadlines. I won't do it." She picked up her statue. "This is it. The last pass I'll get. As of right now, I'm no longer emerging. I'm a wine writer, a critic, a talk-show host, a teacher. I'm competing in a field that's already bursting at the seams. Everyone was nice as could be tonight, but the truth beneath all the smiles is that I've ruffled a lot of feathers becoming a master sommelier before I turn thirty. It'll only get worse if and when I become a master of wine. I'm on a very tall pedestal and they're all waiting for an earthquake."

Donna didn't respond right away. She didn't dismiss the speech out of hand, which Molly had expected. Instead, she nodded. "I can't tell you you're wrong. But I will tell you I wish I'd done a few things differently when I had the chance."

"What do you mean? You love your job."

"That I do. Anyway, none of that matters. You just enjoy your night. You deserve every second of happiness. Now I'm getting the hell out of here. Wayne's drunk, even if he is holding it together well. So I'm gonna send him home and get a good night's sleep. And here comes your knight in an elegant tux. Have fun, and don't forget to use protection."

"Donna!"

"What? I'm just saying."

They both stood as Cam returned, and Donna said something to him that Molly couldn't hear. A few people stopped to congratulate her. By the time they'd moved on, she'd been asked to act as sommelier at a big-deal benefit hosted by the governor and to participate in a wine-tasting fundraiser for Hurricane Sandy victims. Great for her career. But horrible for her clothing budget and overtaxed nerves. Not that she could afford to decline a single invitation. Networking was a huge part of the game.

Donna had obviously heard and gave her an excited smile as she steered Wayne toward the door. Cameron, bless him, had waited patiently off to the side. Now that he could get to her, he moved in and touched her back. The warm pressure of his palm helped her relax.

"You ready to go? Or do you want to stick around and schmooze with your fans?"

"No." She laughed and grabbed her bag while he picked up her award. It was late. In fact, she didn't dare think of what that meant for her class tomorrow. Especially knowing what still lay ahead.

Cam kissed her sweetly. Her lips parted and his tongue slipped past them, but it didn't go much farther. When he pulled away, she wanted to yank him back, but there were too many people around.

Instead of offering his arm, as he'd done on the way in, he took her hand. Although they'd touched all throughout the evening, holding hands seemed more intimate. It was something a guy did with a girlfriend.

He wasn't that, but he'd helped her feel safe tonight. Certainly she could have come alone, and she'd have bumbled her way through the chitchat. It wasn't only something she'd done many times before, but something she needed to practice. She couldn't ask Cameron to be her escort for the rest of her life.

The thought caught her so entirely off guard that she stopped walking.

"You okay?"

She nodded, even managed a smile. But her body wasn't okay. It was buzzing and yearning, not for sex, which would be understandable, but for the way Cameron made her feel.

When they were stalled by the crowd at the exit doors, he rubbed a tiny circle on her wrist with his thumb, and she knew that she *totally* wanted to have sex with Cameron.

How had this one-night stand become so confusing?

It was supposed to be the most sensible, simplest way to satisfy her needs—no strings attached.

If she slept with him, there was a good chance things could end there and they'd never see each other again. On the other hand, if she slept with him, he might want to see her again.

If they continued to see each other, her life was bound to get complicated. But it would also mean he'd be around to escort her to all the functions that seemed to be landing in her lap. With him at her side, she could see herself taking risks in the social arena, which could mean the difference between making her mark in the wine business and ending up as a footnote.

"Molly?"

They were on the street, and she only vaguely remembered getting there. "Hmm?"

Cam gestured to the bellman, waiting for her to enter a taxi. Embarrassed that she hadn't been paying attention, she hurried to duck into the cab, which wasn't easy in her gown. Cameron followed, but only after he'd slipped the doorman a five.

"I imagine you're pretty exhausted," he said. "All that attention and excitement."

"I guess I am." She laid her head back. "But mostly I'm relieved it's over."

"Not for long. I counted three invitations to future events, and I suspect quite a few more will be coming your way. But at least you won't have to do any more speeches."

Molly laughed. "That was the easy part."

"You did pull that off well, which, you do realize, isn't how that usually works with most people."

"Yes, I am painfully aware of that." She brought her head up. "Believe me, I'd rather be able to wade through the small talk without getting tongue-tied."

He brushed the side of her cheek with the backs of his fingers. "You were terrific tonight, all the way around. I had a great time."

"You did, didn't you?"

His chuckle was warm and soft. "Yeah. It was different from the kinds of gatherings I've gone to lately. And you were right about the wine. I was trying to figure out how to sneak some of those bottles home, but I suppose they'd have frowned at that."

It was her turn to laugh. "Donna's got that covered. The bottles really are up for grabs. No one shop gets to resell them, so the U.S. publications tend to divvy up the spoils. We're not the biggest kid on the block, but we'll get our share. Don't worry. I'll make sure you get at least one bottle of something great."

"Use your new clout to get something you like, and we can drink it together."

She turned and stared at him, wishing she could see his face better in the semidarkness. Was he only making conversation, doing that small-talk thing he did so well? Or was he seriously thinking about a next time for them?

"You okay?"

Before she could respond or make her heart stop pounding, her cell phone buzzed.

It had to be Phillip and Simone.

She knew they couldn't have forgotten about tonight. "I'm sorry but I have to take this," she said, fumbling with her ridiculously tiny purse.

When she produced her cell, the name displayed on the caller ID startled her. It was Roxanne. Molly tried to stanch the flow of disappointment coming from deep inside her. She couldn't answer, not now, not without fearing her voice might betray her. Keeping her head down, she tucked the phone back into her purse.

"I really don't mind if you take the call," Cam said.

Molly shook her head. "No. That's okay. It's not who I was expecting."

He slid his arm behind her back and pulled her closer. "That look on your face had me worried for a minute."

She let her head drop to his shoulder. "No need for that. I'd say tonight was a resounding success, and we still have much to look forward to."

The way he exhaled told her a lot. That he hadn't been sure they were going up to her apartment or that anything would happen between them once they got there.

An hour ago she'd been so sure she was going to sleep with him. He'd been the perfect date in every respect. Capping the night off with sex would've been the perfect ending to a perfect evening. But now she wasn't sure anymore.

She feared that trying to make more out of tonight, or out of Cameron, would only end in another disappointment. And she'd had enough of those to last a lifetime.

7

MOLLY'S APARTMENT WAS pretty warm despite the valiant efforts of the window air-conditioning unit. That meant things were going to get sticky. Which wasn't a bad thing, except... Cam looked at the kitchen shower and realized the nozzle would probably reach his shoulder. Oh, well. Compared to the fact that he was here with Molly and that they would soon be getting naked and sweaty, a lousy shower wasn't a big deal.

At least he hoped they'd soon be naked. Something was bothering her and he had no idea what. He was fairly certain it had nothing to do with him. Her mood shift had happened around the time of that call she hadn't answered. But if something really had been wrong, he doubted she'd have invited him up.

"I have iced coffee in the fridge," she said, putting her award in the center of the only table in the place. "I also have wine and a few bottles of beer. Instant iced tea. Maybe a soda..."

She opened the little fridge and he got a decent view of the interior. Mostly beverages and yogurt.

"I think I've had enough wine for the night. I wouldn't say no to some caffeine, though. Iced tea would work."

"Great. Um, just let me get out of this dress."

She was already heading toward her dresser, and Cam's spirits took a dive. He'd imagined undressing her, letting down her hair. Like something right out of a Bond movie. He watched as she selected something from the dresser before moving over to the closet. Looking away before she could turn, he let his gaze roam around her apartment, but his thoughts didn't move on from the nervous vibes he'd felt in the cab.

He didn't think it could be about the sex. Not after the night they'd had. It was probably something simple, like the letdown that often hit after a big event. Hell, her award was a coup that he'd understood only after her speech. Donna had explained the prestige of it—how many emerging wine writers there were out there. But then, he'd known Molly was special since their first date. Maybe she was thinking about the invitations she'd gotten tonight. That schedule of hers was already packed to the rafters.

When the bathroom door shut behind her, he removed his tux jacket, grateful to have it off. Next came his tie, which he stuffed in the jacket pocket, and a few buttons at the collar and cuffs, which he rolled up. He was still warm, and taking his shirt off would've felt even better, but he wasn't about to jump the gun.

The bathroom faucet was running, so he explored a bit, stopping at her bed. God help him, he really wanted to be with Molly. To taste her, make her beg to come…

What the hell was wrong with him? While no one had ever accused him of being Mr. Sensitive, he wasn't a jerk, either. She was calling the shots tonight, and being rock hard when she walked out of the bathroom might send the wrong message. His gaze landed on the cupboards above her headboard and he tried to refocus his thoughts. Built-ins in this place? Maybe the building had been something else before it was turned into closet-sized studio apartments.

The water in the bathroom turned off, raising the pulse

he'd just managed to slow down. As he stared at the bathroom door, willing it to open already, another thought occurred to him.

She'd never said anything about her family. If he was getting an accolade as significant as Molly's, his entire family would have been there to support him. They always had been. Starting with his first school play when he was eight. He'd played a French fry. There had been science fairs, debates, math Olympics, everything up to and including his graduation from MIT. No one had been there for her tonight, except for her coworkers and him. Maybe the call she'd been expecting was from her folks.

He thought about asking Molly if he was right, but the fact that he had to consider it stopped him. It wasn't any of his business. Tonight might have been one of the best nights he'd had in years, but that didn't change the facts: neither one of them was looking for anything more than what was already on offer, and that meant keeping things light. He hadn't even brought up his real work. Why get into all that when it was alcohol they had in common?

The bathroom door opened and he held his breath. She wasn't naked, but that had been a lot to hope for. Instead, she wore a little floral dress. It had spaghetti straps, which he could identify by name because he had four sisters. She'd taken down her hair, which was also disappointing, but not a deal breaker. Not when the look of her, barefoot and leggy, with wide eyes and plush lips, made his cock twitch.

"Hey," he said.

"Hey. Sorry I took so long. Taking off the makeup wasn't as easy as you'd think."

"I can't imagine," he said. "But before you go back to Macy's, you should know you look just as beautiful right now." Her newly bare skin made it easier to see her blush.

"Thanks. You look hot."

"Thanks."

"No," she said, grabbing her gown, already in a plastic bag, and taking it over to her closet. "I mean you looked overheated."

"I am, but you could have let me hold on to my illusions, at least for a little while."

"You think I don't think you're gorgeous?" She opened the closet, and it was as small as he'd expected. When she turned back to him, her hands were on her hips. "Because I believe I mentioned that already."

He shrugged. "Dudes like hearing that stuff, too."

"Really?"

Her teasing renewed his hopes of getting naked. "So you meant that I should remove this tuxedo for my health?"

Instead of returning the banter, she stalled, lips parted, her hands lowered and her gaze looking anywhere but at him. The warning bells went off, and Cam tried to figure out what he'd done to ruin the moment.

Her smile returned, but it wasn't the same as a minute ago. Nope, something had definitely gone south. "How about I fix us those cold drinks first, and then maybe we could talk a minute?"

"Sure," he said, not liking where this was headed. "Is there anything I can do to help?"

"Just tell me how you like your tea."

"No sugar. No lemon."

She walked past him and busied herself with fixing a glass of powdered tea. He considered coming right out and asking if she wanted him to leave. Maybe this had all been some kind of ploy just to get him to take her to the banquet. Or maybe she'd just changed her mind and didn't want to sleep with him after all.

The noise of her stirring the tea was loud and frenetic. He doubted she typically used so much force, or she wouldn't have any glasses left in the cupboard.

"Molly?"

The noise stopped so abruptly, it was as if a door had slammed shut. "I'm sorry," she said. "I've made this a million times more awkward than it needs to be."

"You could just tell me what's on your mind. Whatever it is, I'm pretty sure I won't freak out."

"I might," she said and rolled her eyes. "That wasn't helpful. Look, maybe you could have a seat? The chair looks rickety but it's strong."

"Sure." He took the far chair, the one closest to the exit. She brought his glass over, then sat across from him.

"You don't want a drink?"

She shook her head. "Not right now. Too nervous. I'm just gonna… Okay. Here's the thing. I think you're great. Really great. You've been amazing in every way, but you were unbelievable at the banquet. There aren't enough words to tell you how much it meant to me to have you there. I was scared out of my wits, and you made me feel comfortable and at ease. Tonight was better than I could have ever imagined because of you."

"That's a good thing, right?"

"A very, very good thing. You know what?" She extended her hand over the table. "Could I have a quick sip?"

He handed her the glass. She took a big swig, then handed it back.

"I was telling Donna," she continued, "that tonight I've crossed a threshold. I'm officially in the big leagues. No more passes because I'm young or haven't been around a long time. Getting this far was the hardest thing I've ever done, and now the pressure doubles. I can't have anything distracting me."

"Including me."

She closed her eyes as she sighed, and it was such a

shaky sound that he put his tea down without taking a drink. "Not exactly," she said. "But you're right at the line."

It finally registered. What he'd said. About the two of them drinking the bottle of wine Donna scored for them. He'd made an assumption he had no business making. They hadn't agreed there would be a next time. But it wasn't as if he'd asked her for a date. He was being polite, making an offhanded comment. "The problem is, I like you so much. And I think you like me, too. The kissing has been…" She looked away, her cheeks pink and her eyes shadowed. "Kissing you has been the best. Ever. The thought of us having sex… Well, that's where things become problematic."

"I think I understand what you're saying here." He looked up at the ceiling. "Nope. I don't. Not clear at all. What are you saying?"

"That I'd love, more than anything, if we could take things slower. You know, just be friends for a while."

Man, had he been off the mark. What happened to the whole one-night-stand concept? Surprisingly, despite his desire to keep things simple, he still wanted to see her again. He liked her. But… "Are you talking about dating?"

"No, not— Well, sort of…but not. I don't know what to call it."

"Can you just clarify one thing? Are we talking friends with benefits here?"

"No," she said so abruptly he tried not to take offense. She inhaled as if she hadn't breathed in a while. "I think we had a good time tonight, even without the sex thing, right?"

Cam sighed. Not what he wanted to hear. He drank the rest of the tea. It was terrible. "Go ahead. Finish your spiel. You like me but you see me more like a brother…."

Molly let out a startled laugh. "I don't have a brother, but if I did—" her cheeks filled with color "—I wouldn't kiss him the way I kissed you."

His relief was almost worth the confusion. "A minute ago you were worried about me being a distraction. I would think that would mean you'd want to have sex then cut me loose or show me the door right now."

She smiled a little and sighed. "I'm making a mess of this. Yes, I want to see you again, but it's the sex that's a problem. That's the distraction I'm worried about."

"Um, you don't think not having it could be worse?"

"Not really." She thought for a moment. "Maybe. But I'm not saying we won't ever have sex. I'm sure that eventually we will. Just not yet."

Cam stared at his glass. He probably should've asked for some wine. "In the meantime, we'd sort of be dating, but not, even though your schedule is already insane."

She nodded, her gaze resting on his face. "Those invitations I received tonight, for instance. We could go to those events together."

Ah, here it was. Her endgame. He didn't know if he was more pissed, surprised or hurt. "You know you can always hire an escort. They're even in the yellow pages."

"No. It's not like that, Cam. I think we both know we've got chemistry. Which is great, because being with you is fantastic. But there's that line."

"The distraction line. Right. I forgot. Clothes on, all's good, and we can be pals. Clothes off? Straight to the danger zone. Is that it?"

She stared at him, and he could tell she hadn't liked his descriptions. But he'd lost his sense of humor about this. Not that she owed him anything; she didn't. He just wasn't sure he could deal with a platonic friendship with her. He'd wanted her since the moment they'd met. And while he didn't want to believe she'd played him, he really didn't know her that well.

"No, you're right. It was a dumb thing to ask for," she

said. "I mean, I picked your card because you wanted a one-night stand. I am so sorry." She stood up, nearly toppling her chair, then practically ran back to the counter, where she grabbed another glass and started fixing another glass of iced tea. Her back wasn't to him, but she wasn't looking his way, either.

Maybe that was his cue to leave?

No. Even if she wanted him to, he wasn't going to walk out yet. Not before he gave this whole mess more thought. Found some clarity. Because when she'd said they had chemistry, she wasn't wrong. In fact, she was a little too right about a number of things. Especially about the two of them crossing the line. Maybe she was afraid something big could happen between them. The woman had every minute of her life planned out. She had no room for a relationship, and if she'd felt a spark… Yep, fear could make her back off.

If he'd been thinking with his brain instead of his dick, he'd have realized that he'd gone pretty far out of his way to accommodate a woman he'd been with for a couple of hours. They'd had one dinner together. Admittedly, it had been a remarkable dinner, and each phone conversation after that had added to his desire to see her again, but he was pretty damn sure it wasn't *that* kind of chemistry. That was something different. What he had with Molly was…

He wasn't sure, but it wasn't the forever kind of chemistry. This was crazy chemistry. Complicated. Full of pitfalls and way too little getting naked. Then again, he wasn't even going to be here in a few months, so maybe it wouldn't be so terrible to go with her to her banquets and whatever.

"You want to leave, don't you."

He jerked in his seat and found her standing right next to him. Holding another glass of terrible tea. "No," he said. Then he took the tea and drank a bunch. It wasn't any better than the first glass. "I'm thinking."

"Oh."

"It's a lot to process."

She sat down again. "Yes. Please. Think as long as you'd like."

"Thanks," he said, thinking that he had better not look at her while he was trying to figure this out, because whatever else was true, he still wanted her like crazy. Which was the crux of the matter. Could he escort her to another event, knowing there would be no...? "What about kissing?" he asked.

"Oh," she said again, sounding a little surprised. "I don't know. I really like kissing you."

He nodded. Thought about saying something, but for the life of him couldn't figure out what. So he tried to imagine himself with her, if kissing was part of the deal.

Oh, hell, he'd had plenty of dates that hadn't ended in the bedroom. None of which had been half as much fun as talking on the phone to Molly. That wasn't to say he was willing to roll over and be a doormat. She wanted them to be platonic friends who might eventually have sex? Fine. Then it would be his job to help her see that sooner was better than later. While still letting her set the pace, of course. "You know what? There might be a way this could work."

She sat up straighter. "Oh?"

"You know how I told you my sisters are a pain in my ass?"

That made her blink. "Yeah?"

"They keep wanting to set me up with women who want to get married. I don't want to get married. At least not now." He leaned over the table, his hands wrapped around the cold glass as condensation dripped down the sides. "So let's posit that I do accompany you to your...things. What if you, in turn, come to some things with me?"

"What kinds of things do you mean?"

"The nature of the things isn't the important part."

"What is?"

"You have to act like you're my girlfriend."

She looked at him very seriously. For a long while. Finally, she said, "So they stop setting you up with women who want to get married."

He smiled.

"And in return, you accompany me to some events." She sat back, looked up at the cottage-cheese ceiling.

He almost laughed. Seemed they both used staring at the ceiling to think through problems.

"You'll always be assured of great wine," she said, "and usually great food."

"That's a plus," he said. "And when you're with me, you'll get to indulge in your secret beer habit."

She smiled as she met his gaze. "Can we leave the kissing as is for the time being?"

"Sure."

"And we'll just play it out. See how it goes?"

"Precisely."

She held out a hand, and he took it.

"One more thing," he said. "Since we're just friends, there shouldn't be a problem with me seeing other women. Right?"

He didn't miss her flinch or the silent gasp formed by her lips. He did everything he could not to let his satisfaction show. He wasn't trying to hurt her or be cruel. But he had to know he wasn't being the biggest chump in five boroughs. And that she felt the same spark he did.

"I thought you wanted to avoid being set up."

"True. On the other hand…"

"Right. The trading cards." She blinked a few times and gave him a strained smile. "Of course."

"It appears we have a deal," he said. Then he got up, grabbed his tuxedo jacket from the back of her chair and went to the door.

"You're leaving?"

"I am. Mostly because I'm getting hard again, and that's counterproductive. Also, because we both need to think this through."

"Of course," she said. She stood up and crossed her arms over her chest. "I appreciate this."

He opened the door, but before he left, he made sure she was looking straight into his eyes. "You do realize the chances of us not breaking down and just going at it are really small. I know you think it could be dangerous, but I don't agree. I think it will *definitely* get dangerous." He figured his smile would tell her that he wasn't a man to back down when things got challenging.

Her lips parted, and there it was…barely a whisper. "Oh."

He shut the door firmly behind him.

8

MOLLY TURNED OFF the intercom between herself and the engineer's booth. Today wasn't going well. And not just in a Wednesday kind of way.

As she'd feared, Cameron was already a distraction. Since he'd walked out of her apartment Friday night, she'd thought of him—of them—so many times that she'd been distracted at her two Saturday wine classes, done an amateurish job at the tasting in Chelsea and would probably have to completely scratch every idea she'd had for her next column.

What she needed to do right now was put Cameron in a box. It was a trick a therapist had taught her years ago, when she'd been having problems with bullies in middle school. The technique was in large part responsible for her getting through life. The idea was to gain control over whatever was bothering her, which, in this case, was Cameron. It was important to visualize the issue or object very clearly. Notice the details. Block out everything but that one particular image. Then very carefully shrink it. Him. The whole of him. Shrink them until she could fit them into the small imaginary box in the palm of her hand.

He was almost there. Not quite. He was still too large to fit into the box. In fact, she couldn't even open the box.

What was wrong? She'd never had to pull and tug at the lid before. It was a stupid little box with a hinge opening. The same one she always visualized. It wasn't even locked. Or real. And now Cameron was getting bigger. He was still naked, and he wasn't the only thing growing.

Wonderful. Now he was life-size, stark naked and smiling. She could see the smattering of chest hair that became more sparse as it drew her gaze down to his treasure trail, and holy crap, he was hard, and aching, and all she had to do was reach out her—

"Molly!"

She jerked up and opened her eyes to find Roxanne standing in the doorway.

"You're on the air," Roxanne said, her stage whisper as fierce as her glare.

Molly flipped the switches that would bring her back on live and said, "Sorry about that. A bit of a technical issue. We're all good now. Who's our next caller, Bobby?"

"It's Heather from the Bronx, and she wants to know what wine would go well with Vietnamese cuisine."

"Hi, Heather," Molly said, trying to get the afterimage of Cam out of her brain. "Any dish in particular?"

"Hey, hi, Molly. Love the show. I'm making red rice salad with mint. I was going to go with Thai iced tea or Sapporo, but I want to try something different."

Molly smiled. Not because she was happy, but because it would make her sound happy. Another trick she'd learned from her therapist. "I like it. Thinking outside the box—" she winced at her unfortunate choice of words "—is a great idea when you're planning a daring meal. I'd say Sauvignon Blanc, Viognier and white Burgundies are all great choices. There are a lot of pungent fresh herbs you're dealing with, like mint, cilantro and parsley, and many experts swear that they're made for a decent Sauv Blanc.

Which also goes with the cool cucumber in the salad. Or you could try a dry Rosé, sparkling wine or a Frascati. All of those are great picnic drinks that pair well with salads."

"I like Sauvignon Blanc," Heather said. "Any personal favorites?"

"Give the Sterling Vineyards a try. It's only around twelve dollars a bottle."

"Sounds great. Thanks. And keep up the good work!"

"You're welcome," Molly said, holding on to her smile for dear life because she was not only distracted but filled with regret. The whole concept of not sleeping with Cameron was idiotic. He was gorgeous and wonderful. Besides, those last words he'd said to her had been following her like a shadow, taunting her, and sounding more appealing by the hour. She'd avoided danger all her life, so why did it sound so exciting now?

"Next up, we've got George from NYU's Broome Street residence hall," Bobby said.

Molly listened with her eyes on the clock as George meandered through his question. She could be enthusiastic about a wine pairing for Frito pie. She could. Ten more minutes, and the program would be over. Frito pie was like a tamale, and tamales were spicy. "I'd recommend a German Riesling, which is amazing with spicy foods because the sugar in the wine helps to counteract the spice. The wine's fruit flavors are set off by the corn and pork filling of the tamale." She went on, giving him other choices and prices and everything she could pull from her memory bank, because this was important.

Because if she couldn't get her eye back on the prize, Cameron would have to go. Completely.

HE WAS SUPPOSED to be working on the cream ale. Or having lunch. Or both. Instead, Cam was sitting at his lab table staring at the ceiling. It was more of a storage closet than a lab, but he supposed the place where he made small batches of what were basically home-brew experiments could be considered a lab. Today, however, he hadn't done a single experiment. In fact, the only thing he'd accomplished was returning his tuxedo to the rental place. And thinking about Molly.

Jesus. He'd been so close. Moments away from having a perfect night. He should have just kissed her. Swept her into his arms and led her to the bed. Chased away all that logic and fear by making her wet and aching and... God, he was shallow. Sex wasn't that important. Shouldn't be. But with Molly? It seemed vital. Like the need for oxygen or gravity.

He groaned as his head dropped into his hands. Shallow, horny, confused. That was him in a nutshell. He'd been horny since puberty, so that wasn't a surprise, and he was confused more often than not when it came to women. But he'd always considered himself someone his sisters would approve of. That his current thoughts were nothing more than a loop of increasingly filthy images of him and Molly ruining the sheets was troubling.

He pulled out his cell, but instead of calling Molly, he dialed his boss. Ex-boss. Future boss. Dr. Inaba was the senior biochemist in charge of Cam's team at Protean Pharmaceuticals. She'd been his thesis adviser at MIT and she'd asked him to work with her on finding something that would crack the biochemical code for resistant antibiotics.

"Cam. I was going to call you."

"Have you heard anything?"

"Nothing concrete, no. But the government task force is moving at a steady, albeit achingly slow, pace. Unless something dramatic happens, I'm thinking three, four months before it goes to committee. With the new reports coming out from the World Health Organization, things should be scary enough to stop politicizing the issue, and it should move quickly through a vote."

"Wow, what a thing to hope for."

"Yeah," she said. "Frankly, I can't wait to get back to it. I'm buried in paperwork and I miss the team."

"So do I."

"At least you get to do fun things like make beer while you're gone."

He grinned. Dr. Inaba was a major beer fan. They'd originally met when she'd come to his dorm room at MIT to try one of his small brews. "I'll ship you a case or two to hold you over."

"Excellent news. I'll let you know when I hear anything at all."

Cameron hung up, glad that things were moving forward. Three, four months had to be enough time for Molly to come to her senses. Good God, he'd never live through one month, let alone four.

He jotted down a note to send Dr. Inaba a case of the new lambic and one of Irish red. He knew she liked the latter and was pretty certain the lambic would hit the spot.

Molly had really liked the Cabernet Sauvignon at the banquet. He had, as well, but she'd been downright excited about it. And she'd said something that had been niggling at him, at least when he took a second to think of anything else but having sex with her. She'd said she'd liked the astringent mouthfeel. Huh. He wondered if she liked Indian pale ales. The American double, in particular.

He'd have to ask. Or better yet, give her some. He thought of their India pale ales, and while they were great, they weren't exactly what he was thinking of.

He turned the page in his notebook and started listing what he'd need to make a perfect India pale ale for Molly.

He'd have to do some research on Cabernet Sauvignon, make sure he could mimic as much as possible what she liked about the wine. It would have to be bold, with black currant notes, mint, a smoky aroma and some oak.

When he looked up again, it was almost seven o'clock and he had a basic recipe outlined, complete with the hop percentage and the kind of malt he figured would give him the best result.

It would take a while to lock it down and at least a few weeks to make it. If they hadn't slept with each other by then, he could always use the fermentation tank to drown himself.

Until then, his stomach required food but, more important, he needed something physical to do. He'd been sleeping like crap, and he'd be damned if he was going to go through another lousy night. Luckily, The Four Sisters served food.

About three minutes later he was in the kitchen of their taproom, and while they didn't have a large menu, the stuff they had was excellent. Especially the bratwurst and sauerkraut. And the pulled-pork sandwich. Hell, maybe he'd even get some mac and cheese to go with his newest porter. He made himself a combo platter and ate it too quickly in the manager's office.

"Stealing food again?"

Cam looked up, his mouth full and still chewing, as his dad walked in. He was wearing a green Four Sisters T-shirt, as always, with his jeans and his steel-toed boots. He looked tired. Nothing unusual there.

When he was able to talk, Cam gave a nod toward the taproom. "It's like the old days. I don't think there's an open seat."

Gordon sank onto the small couch that rested under a shuttered window. "I don't know why we bothered. It's damn hard work when there are actual customers."

"Yeah. What were we thinking?"

They shared a smile that went all the way back to the very first time the two of them brewed beer together. Cameron had been too young to add anything but enthusiasm to the process, but home brewing had been their thing. Still was. No girls were allowed, and for Cam, that was huge. Almost as big a deal as the fact that they'd grown close over those home brews. Stayed close. It also happened to be where Cameron had first fallen in love with chemistry.

Which was just the kind of thing he'd end up telling Molly, if he went through with this crazy plan of hers.

"I'm thinking we need to increase our growlers," his dad said. "We ran out last Friday."

"I don't know," Cam replied, taking the last bite of his pulled-pork sandwich. "Maybe running out's a good thing."

Gordon and Cam tossed the notion around, the pros and cons, and when they'd worn that topic down to the nub, they moved on to the brewery's equipment and whether they really needed to replace the old finishing tank.

When Amber came in, it was already ten-thirty. Long past when he could comfortably call Molly. It didn't matter. He'd already decided he was going to talk to her tomorrow, ask her to come to Queens to hold up her part of their bargain. For now, he'd enjoy the time with his dad. Nothing beat face-to-face time with Gordon.

"Have there ever been two lazier men in this world?" Amber asked, shaking her head. "I highly doubt it. There's karaoke suicide being committed out there, and here you two are, gabbing away as if you're on vacation."

Cam rolled his eyes, but he forced himself to get up and face the music—an excellent punishment for slacking off on his duties, especially when Kelly Tobin was torturing the soul out of a Rod Stewart ballad.

The rest of the night went by in a beer-scented blur. On nights he worked till closing, he was always immensely grateful for the apartment above the bar. On nights he needed to go to sleep early, he cursed the location and the inadequacy of soundproofing. He used earplugs, but that didn't stop the walls from shaking.

Still, the apartment was private and free and it meant he didn't have to stay at his dad's house. Not that he had a problem with his dad. But Amber lived there now, and for some reason his other sisters and the neighbors felt the need to drop by at random whenever Gordon was home. It drove Cam crazy. He was sociable, but there were limits.

Here, at least most of the time, he could think. And dream.

Before he went to bed he thought about Molly coming to the bar. His old man would like her, and he was pretty sure, if they could get to talking about spirits, Molly would like him right back.

And maybe, just maybe, she'd like Cam's bed, too.

MOLLY STOOD ON the sidewalk outside The Four Sisters. It was almost eight o'clock and she'd had to ask a friend to take over her Thursday evening wine class. Something she'd done only twice before, both times when she'd been sick and contagious. Considering Cameron's willingness to escort her to a tasting Saturday afternoon, she had no business resenting this trip to Queens.

Okay, it wasn't so much resentment as terror. Not only because she'd be meeting his family and pretending to be his girlfriend, which was intimidating enough, but she'd never been able to shrink Cameron to a size she could handle. He continued to loom large in her thoughts, making her life increasingly difficult.

"Be brave," she whispered, hoping the thought would take root. She'd been to scarier things than a brewpub. For heaven's sake, she'd gone to six different schools by the time she was fifteen.

The whole trip over, she'd tried convincing herself that this was going to be excellent practice, both in improving her interpersonal skills and in testing her ability to control herself. Because, naturally, there would be kissing involved.

Kissing with an eye toward convincing people who had literally grown up with Cam that they were getting serious.

A couple of guys wearing bandannas around their foreheads and black Harley-Davidson T-shirts headed into the bar. As the door swung open, Molly heard the murmur of the crowd and the high-pitched climax to a Journey song.

This had disaster written all over it.

She'd call him, make up some kind of excuse. Her train had broken down. It happened all the time. Anyone would believe that, especially in this heat wave.

Or she could tell him the deal was off. That would ensure that she'd never have to come back here again. Never meet his sisters. His father. Never kiss him again or lean against his broad chest with his arm keeping her close. Never smell his masculine scent with its hint of hops that made her mouth water. Never see his smile or the way he looked at her as if she was the best thing he'd seen in ages.

The door opened again, and Molly decided she'd take a quick walk. Get focused. Cameron knew her shortcomings. He wasn't the kind of man to ignore them. He'd never throw her into a situation she couldn't handle. He had a lot riding on tonight. The man most definitely didn't want a committed relationship if he was willing to go to these lengths. And marriage? No way.

His trading card had given her all the information she needed about Cam. His passion was beer. She liked beer. The whole family worked in the industry. They'd talk about beer.

She realized she hadn't moved at all in five minutes. Time to fix that. She hated being late.

After two deep breaths, she pulled open the heavy green door and stepped inside Cameron's world.

9

CAMERON HADN'T TRULY believed she would come until he saw her. He'd given this plan a great deal of thought. He wanted her to see the pub, how big it was. How crowded and noisy. But he didn't want her meeting anyone yet.

Since he'd been hovering near the entrance for the past ten minutes, he was at her side in seconds, had her hand in his a moment later and steered her outside before she could catch her breath.

"What are you doing?"

"Taking you up to my apartment."

She stopped. "Why?"

"Prep work. I wanted you to see the environment first."

"Oh, God."

When he started walking again she followed, thank goodness, but not quickly enough. "It's not going to be that bad. Promise." By the time they reached his place, she was flushed, and he didn't think it was because of the heat.

"Cold drink?"

She nodded.

"Beer? Soda?"

"I'll save the alcohol for the bar."

"Good idea." He split a can of cola, which was all he had. She didn't seem to mind.

Within a minute her color softened and her breathing had returned to normal as she scoped out the apartment. "It's big," she said.

"Only compared to your shoebox."

She turned her face up to him. "That's true."

"You done with that soda?" he asked, not giving her a chance to answer before he put both their glasses on the counter. Then he pulled her close, finally getting to kiss her.

For a second, she stiffened. But only for a second. Then she was melting against him, kissing him back with the same eagerness she'd exhibited the night of the banquet. The thrust of her tongue made him ache for so much more, he actually considered backing off.

But the hell with that. Not when her hand was running down his back, when the feel of her body lit him up like a neon sign blinking *YES*. He'd imagined this and so much more, and now that he had her, he didn't want to share. Not with his family, not with the bar. If he could, he'd lock her inside his apartment for the rest of the night.

She pulled away, catching her breath, and smiled, and even through her unmistakable desire, he could see her nervousness.

He longed to comfort her, preferably in bed, but he had to be on point, at least for a while. Long enough for them to face the three sisters who were currently downstairs working. The good part was that Emmy already knew about Molly, so he wouldn't have to exaggerate too much about their relationship—which was also, now that he thought about it, the bad part.

"Don't look like that," she said. "I'm worried enough on my own."

There would be more kissing. Later. Touching, sooner. If they could pull this thing off. "Right," he said, letting her go. "The family."

Her arms dropped slowly, stopping first to line up the buttons on her pale green blouse. She'd worn jeans, and he hadn't seen her in anything that casual yet. It was nice. In fact, he'd love to get her into a Four Sisters T-shirt. Everything about her looked as put together as she'd been on their first date. A far cry from the little flowered sundress he remembered so vividly.

"So, do you call your sister Emerald or Emmy?" she asked.

"Emmy," he said, getting his head into the game. "Then there's Ruby, my oldest sister. She won't be here tonight. She's the one who lives in Indiana. She's married, and they have a little boy, Trevor, who is the coolest two-year-old on the planet. Anyway, you will be meeting Amber, who lives at our old house with my dad, and Jade, who manages the business. They all know who you are, and that we met via the trading-card thing, but they don't know anything about our relationship. Emmy knows I went with you to the banquet. That's it."

"What about your dad?"

"His name is Gordon. And he probably doesn't have a clue."

Molly looked up for a moment, most likely digesting the situation. When she turned her attention back to him, she asked, "Am I supposed to be me? Or different?"

The question knocked him a little sideways. "No, not someone different. The whole reason this can work is because they'd all completely believe you are someone I'd fall for."

Molly's face was a picture of stunned confusion, but she cleared her throat and gave him a short nod. Cameron handed her back the little bit of cola that she'd left in her glass.

"Okay," she said, after polishing off the soda. "In this make-believe scenario that we're acting out for the benefit of your family, are we lovers?"

"I can't imagine that'll come up, but it's your call," he said, as rapidly as he could spit out the words.

"No. No, we're not. We're taking it slow. Very slow."

"I know. Don't rub it in," he said with a wink and ignored the smile she was trying to hide. She handed him her glass, and he put it in the sink with his own. "Ready?"

Molly patted her back pockets, took out a small tube of lipstick, swiped it on her lips, then put the tube back. "I look okay? Nothing open that should be closed?"

"You look gorgeous."

"Wish me luck." She walked out to the landing, but stopped in front of the door to the bar. "If you see me cough behind my hand, rescue me."

"Got it. Coughing behind your hand is the signal. Oh, one more thing you should know." He stopped, his hand on the door pull. "I don't really brew beer for a living."

THE BAR WAS bigger on the inside. In fact, it was huge, and it was full of people, and it was loud. She pulled on a smile, hoping it would do more than make her sound happy.

Nope. She was still reeling.

He was a chemist? A PhD? Part of a pharmaceutical research team? Who'd waited until two minutes ago to tell her?

She had so many questions, and he'd left her no time to ask them. Yet he'd still managed to point out that they were really only casual friends and their relationship was little more than a business arrangement so far. So, everything was cool, right?

Then he'd walked her through the door.

To meet his family.

Cameron's arm went around her waist. She jumped a little, then leaned against him as she'd done at the awards banquet. It worked like a charm. While it didn't remove her anxiety or assuage her confusion, the comfort of his embrace gave her the courage to take the next step forward.

"You okay?"

"So far," she said.

"How about we get some beers, then take a look at our options?"

She smiled up at him. She rarely used alcohol as a social tool. But today? Yes, yes and more yes.

A real honest-to-goodness chemist. Huh. Of course, it changed nothing. But it was surprising.

"Come look at what we have on tap. You can have your pick of the crop."

They walked along the edge of the crowd, past numerous tables, some made of wood, others of plastic, all of them round. The chairs were random, mismatched. Few tables were empty, and many of them were pulled together to cater to larger groups.

It was definitely more laid-back than any wine bar she'd been to. It made her think of neighborhood pubs from television or books. More like the dive bars she'd gone to in college. That she'd stopped going to in college when her grades started to suffer. And there was another helpful reminder that getting too comfortable with Cam was not in her best interest.

Helping him with his matchmaking sisters was.

"What do you think?" he asked, slowing them down until they stopped a few feet from the huge wooden bar.

She took in as much of the room as she could. The walls were brick, painted either red or white. The artwork was eclectic. On one wall there were old beer signs, on another, what looked like local art. The heart of the tap-room, though, was the bar itself. It was appropriately long, with a well-stocked display of spirits against a big mirror. To the left of that was the main attraction: maybe seventy bottles of unique beers stacked on a wooden shelf. Below that, a tap tower that served a dozen brews, and a hustling staff, all dressed in green Four Sisters T-shirts. The employees were a mixed bag, including a couple of men who appeared to be in their fifties— Oh, God, one of them was probably Cam's father.

The taller of the two men turned her way, and that was him, of course. Same good looks, aged beautifully. It was like a peek into Cam's future. She'd known only a few people who resembled their parents as much.

Cam squeezed her waist and nodded at a tall woman with a long braid pouring a draft. "That's Jade. It's not hard to identify my clan. All the womenfolk in my family are around six feet."

"You and your dad look very much alike."

"So I've been told." He pulled her into his arms and rocked her back and forth. Slowly, in contrast to Beyoncé's "Single Ladies," which blasted out of the jukebox.

When he released her, he didn't let her go. Instead, he captured her lips. Sweetly, slowly. No tongue. Just lips on lips, soft, kind, rekindling the ache low in her stomach, between her thighs. Pulling back, his gaze lingered as his smile grew. "Come on. Let's go meet my old man."

"Okay," she said and pulled up the smile that always saved her on the radio.

The braided sister, Jade, had stopped pouring drinks and stood staring at the two of them unabashedly, a pint of dark beer in her hand. Without turning, she leaned to her right and said something Molly couldn't hear. Cameron's father spun around, and now there were two people staring at them.

"Dad, Jade, come out here," Cam said, shouting to be heard. Of course, everyone within fifty feet turned to stare at them. "Someone I want you to meet."

Jade put the glass on the bar so quickly it splashed, and Cam's father wiped his hands on a towel with a grin that was very familiar to Molly. In less time than it would have taken her to run to the exit, she found herself face-to-face with two tall, good-looking people who didn't bother to hide their curiosity at all.

"Now, who's this?" Cam's father asked, sparing the briefest glance at his son.

"Dad, Jade, this is Molly Grainger. Molly, this is my dad, Gordon, and my sister Jade."

There were handshakes. Enthusiastic handshakes. "Good to meet you, Molly," Gordon said. "You must be someone special if he's brought you around to this place."

"Oh, wait, you're the woman from the trading-card thing Emmy's doing." Jade bumped her father's shoulder without turning to him. "Remember Emmy said she'd met a pretty nice guy? What was his name…Jonas? From that group she goes to? That's right, isn't it, Molly?"

"I don't know about Emmy's date, but yes. I met Cameron from his trading card."

"That's been a few weeks now." Jade finally looked at her brother. "You didn't tell us that you were still seeing her."

"As hard as it is to believe, you guys aren't in charge of my social life. Or any other part of my life."

"Now, Cam," Gordon said, "we all have your best interests at heart."

"I appreciate the sentiment. I do. In fact, that's why

Molly has graciously agreed to be here today, despite knowing she'll be grilled like a jewel thief."

"Hey." Jade frowned. "Don't talk to your father like that. Our manners are impeccable."

"I wasn't referring to him. And you might want to stop staring like you'd never seen another human before, huh? Give Molly a break?"

"The solution to this is simple." Gordon stepped back and nodded at a door that led behind the bar, probably to the cooler. "Why don't we find Amber and Emmy and give Molly something to drink. Get to know each other a bit."

Cameron looked at Molly, and from his expression she could tell he wasn't sure what to do. He'd never mentioned a private conversation. Of course, he'd never mentioned being a chemist, either. God. She really had to let that go....

She had enough to worry about with everyone ganging up on her. Oh, Christ. She'd be center stage. They'd want to know about her background, a lot of which she hadn't told Cam. She might've appreciated the irony more if she wasn't ready to bite off every one of her fingernails.

"You know what?" Cam pulled her closer. "I promised her a true Four Sisters experience. We're gonna find ourselves a table—even if we have to bring one of the spares out from the back room—and get some beer and some food, and you guys are free to stop by now and again. Deal?"

Jade looked as if she was ready to argue, but Gordon nodded immediately. "Absolutely. I'll take care of the table. Jade, maybe you can find out what kind of beer Molly would like and we'll go from there."

Molly's relief made her knees wobbly. Now that Cam had laid out the rules, she could breathe again. Take things as they came. She made the first move. "I saw a few people had flights," she said. "I'd love to sample what you have on offer so I can get a real feel for your brews."

Jade nodded. "Come on. I'll get you a couple menus. You're into wine, right?"

"Yep," Molly said, joining her as they headed to the bar, letting Cameron go with his dad, but only because she had to. At least they were talking about alcohol. She couldn't wait to have some of her very own.

"I like wine," Jade said, "especially the reds. A good Merlot, a nice Shiraz. I'll have to quiz you for tips on good buys."

By the time Molly had ordered her pale-ale flight, a round table had been shoved into place for them near the bar. That meant a lot of shuffling from the other patrons, but no one seemed to mind. The minute five chairs were corralled, all of the folding variety and not very comfortable looking, Molly took a seat.

Jade had poured the flight, four different samples of beer on a wooden tray with grooves that held two-ounce glasses. Cameron handed her a menu before he sat down next to her, and Gordon brought back two big glasses of a dark draft for himself and Cam.

It was like living in a montage sequence, all accompanied by Adele on the jukebox.

Cam took a large swig, then gave her a briefing on the ales she was about to taste. At this point, it probably wouldn't have mattered if she was tasting Dom Pérignon White Gold Jeroboam—all she'd be able to discern was wet. This was worse than taking exams. Worse than teaching her very first class.

Then Emmy appeared at the table. It was odd to see her in this context when Molly had met her only in the city. She looked far more relaxed here, which came as no surprise—everyone in the building looked at home. "Molly!" she said, falling into the last empty chair. "I didn't know you were coming. How nice. Cam mentioned you guys were still seeing each other. Cool."

"I think so," Cam said.

"It's good to see you, too, Emmy. How's your luck been with the trading cards?"

Molly couldn't have asked a better question. For the next twenty minutes, Emmy regaled everyone at the table with her story about how she'd been dating a guy, Jonas, who was nice, but not right for her, not for the long run, and how she should've known right away when he told her he didn't much care for beer. That got Gordon talking about how he didn't trust people who didn't like beer, and everyone seemed to have an opinion on that.

Before long, several small plates of pub grub arrived at the table, along with the appropriate accoutrements, and it started to feel to Molly more like a party than an interrogation.

She found herself actually enjoying the beer, enjoying listening to the banter and relaxing into Cam's affectionate touches.

It took her almost an hour to realize no one had asked her much at all, which was strange, and that in her whole life she'd rarely been around a family who got along so well. Certainly never in any of the foster homes or group homes she'd lived in. Even Phillip and Simone, while they'd been wonderful to her, weren't the kind to tease each other or get in each other's faces.

The Crawfords made it look so easy.

Emmy relinquished her chair to Amber, who looked a lot like the other sisters, except that her hair was shorter and streaked with blue, but she ended up hanging around anyway, telling Molly all kinds of interesting tidbits. That she was the second-oldest sister at thirty-seven, and that

Ruby was the oldest at thirty-nine. That Cameron had been a "first-class nerd" growing up, and if Molly wanted a laugh she should get him to play basketball.

"It's okay, though," Amber said. "We forgive him for a lot on account of he's saving the world."

Guessing that had something to do with his being a chemist, Molly looked at Cameron. She could see he wasn't pleased. When he finished glaring at his second-oldest sister, he attempted a smile as he met Molly's gaze. "I'm not saving the world. Eventually, hopefully, we'll save a lot of lives."

"Save lives?"

"I bet he never even told you how important his real job is," Emmy said. "But when his team gets funded, they're going to find a way to outmaneuver the strains of bacteria that have figured out how to resist our antibiotics. I fully expect him to win the Nobel Prize. Eventually. Well, maybe not on his own."

Molly found a smile for him and hoped her face didn't crack with the strain. "No, he hasn't told me nearly enough about his real work."

"Right now, my real work is making beer. Besides, it's not a sure thing that the project will ever get funded."

Gordon put a hand on Cameron's shoulder. "No matter what, though, we should still have you for at least four more months, right?"

Molly had just picked up her beer. Instead of taking a sip, she set it back down before she spilled the whole thing. Well, wasn't Cameron just full of surprises today? His mouth and eyes had tightened. Clearly, he hadn't wanted her to know he was here only temporarily. That he had a separate life. His family's rush to set him up with a wife made a little more sense to her now, she supposed.

She realized she was frowning. Upset more than confused, and that wouldn't do. Her job today was to make them all believe they were a couple. A couple who would tell each other little things, like how they were leaving for God knew where in a few months.

"You want to try another beer?" Cam asked her.

"Yeah, thanks. I would. In fact, I think I'll go up and take a look at the drafts again."

"I'll come with you."

She stood and smiled at him, making sure it reached her eyes. "I'm going to make a pit stop first. Can I get you something else from the bar while I'm there?" She looked around. "Anyone?"

No one took her up on her offer, and she made her way to the restrooms. By the time she was inside, locked in a stall, she'd settled down enough to get some perspective.

Why would he have told her? He was right when he'd said their deal was more business than personal. At her own request. He'd never claimed to be anything but a one-night stand. She'd broken the rules by asking him to stick around. He was under no obligation to fill her in on the details of his life. Or the big picture, for that matter. So why was she so hurt?

Yes, this revelation meant she'd have him as an escort for only a few more months. That was better than not at all, right? The truth didn't have to change their agreement.

Except...

Her heart started to pound.

...in one vital area.

He'd be gone soon. In a matter of months. She wasn't about to fall in love with him that quickly. Especially given that they'd see each other only a dozen times or so, maybe less.

So. It might not be the one-night stand he'd wanted, but it would solve a couple of problems. First, she would continue to be his girlfriend until he went back to his other life. And, far more important, she no longer saw any reason for them to put off having sex.

It will, in essence, be a four-month stand.

Uncomplicated and perfect. A win-win all the way around.

She finished her business and stared into her own gaze as she washed her hands. Now that she understood the parameters, and that there would be no chance of him messing with her future, the ride was about to get a whole lot more interesting.

Lingering, she practiced the smile she was going to give him. For someone who was supposed to be some kind of genius, he sure was a dope. She couldn't wait to see his expression when he realized his error. If he'd told her the truth right off, they would've been tangling up the sheets long before tonight.

10

It was his own fault. He should have said something to Molly about his work in Syracuse sooner. He hadn't given it much thought, actually. What they had in common was this life, not the other. He liked that it was simple with her, that they could have this connection where they understood each other's shorthand.

But she'd been shocked by the news that he was here temporarily, no denying that. The question was, should he feel guilty about it? Apologize? Tell her he was sorry for failing to mention his other career? Ask her to forgive him for not bringing up his still-unsettled future? Nope. The only thing he could feel bad about was the fact that she'd been caught unawares, but that was bound to happen. His sisters had also outed him for being lousy at sports and being a big nerd back in high school. Frankly, that was more upsetting to him.

He caught sight of Molly at the bar and couldn't help admiring the way she looked in her jeans. He didn't want to be in the bar anymore. His plan had worked, and he was reasonably sure the family would ease up on their push to marry him off.

Someday, when he had the job situation settled, he'd

meet the right person with the forever kind of chemistry and the whole situation would resolve itself. He was even more certain of that now. Hell, things felt pretty right with Molly, and she wasn't even the kind of long-term partner he was looking for.

"Cam!"

The sharp note in Amber's voice made him turn back toward the table. "What?"

"I had no idea you liked her this much."

"What do you mean?"

Amber threw a rolled-up piece of napkin at him. "She walks away from the table and you've been in dreamland ever since instead of here with us. I've never seen you act that way before. Is there something you want to share with the class?"

"I like her, okay? A lot. But don't make more of it than there is." He pointed at Amber, then Emmy. "I mean it."

"Yes, sir." Amber saluted, which was annoying. "What I *was* going to say before you didn't hear me call your name four times was that I like her. And that you two are very cute together."

Molly's beer glass hit the table, and then she was leaning over him to steal a kiss. When she sat down again, she grinned at Amber. "I agree."

Cam got very still as he tried to process the past ten minutes. She'd heard his stay in Queens was temporary. She'd come back and kissed him. In a much better and more relaxed mood, no less.

Hypothesis? The new information made her happy. Because she'd be rid of him soon? The quality of her smile had changed. She seemed more animated. But the bare foot that was sneaking underneath his pant leg suggested the answer was something better.... "What's that?" he asked, nodding at her beer. "I'd guess the cream ale, although you're pretty daring, so maybe it's the blond?"

"You were right the first time. I wanted something smooth and easy. I have a busy night ahead."

"Do you?" he asked, lowering his voice as he moved in closer to her.

"You're an idiot," she said, her voice just above a whisper.

"I know," he said. "What for this time?"

"You really don't get it?"

"Give me a hint," he murmured, glad his sisters were busy arguing over a baseball score on the TV screen.

Molly's toes slid higher up his calf. "You should have told me you weren't going to be here long."

"I'm not certain when I'm going. I don't even know when I'll know."

Her right hand landed on his left thigh. "We could have avoided a lot of confusion."

"No," he said, putting it all together. She'd have slept with him already if he'd mentioned Syracuse? "Seriously?"

She grinned.

"Why does my leaving make such a big difference?"

"Come on. Four months? Maybe we'll get together, what, ten, twelve times? How complicated could things get?"

"Huh."

"Yeah."

He stood up, dislodging both her hand and, in a move that nearly caused her to lose her balance, her foot. "We've got to go. You've all been great. See you tomorrow."

Molly's cheeks turned pink, but she didn't seem to mind that he'd said they were leaving. "What about my beer?"

"Take it with you if you want. I can get a growler. I have connections here."

"No, it's fine."

He took her hand and started to pull her away, but she slipped free. "Cam. Give me a minute."

"Cameron," his father said, frowning. "What's gotten into you?"

He might have overdone it there. Lucky for him, Molly was more gracious about saying her goodbyes and didn't appear to be put off by his sisters laughing at him so blatantly or his poor dad's confused expression.

As soon as he and Molly were outside, he kissed her, but not for long. There was much to do upstairs. He doubted they could squeeze in all the things he'd thought of, but they could make a good start.

By the time they reached his door they were both panting and she'd spilled a quarter of her beer. Didn't matter. He'd get her more. He'd get her all the beer. As long as they were inside, and she was his for the night.

NEVER. NOT EVER, ever had there been a man in Molly's life who had wanted her so much.

It was probably the anticipation. For the past couple of weeks she hadn't skipped a night with her vibrator—and she hadn't given as much as a thought to Mr. Cumberbatch. So she supposed she shouldn't feel so flattered that Cameron was more than eager.

But she couldn't deny the thrill that shot through her when she could so clearly see the urgency in his eyes.

His gaze traveled across her face from side to side, up and down. He didn't blink. Not once. Just swallowed, his Adam's apple bobbing up and down. His hand rose but didn't touch her face.

A second later he blinked. And blinked again. Then he laughed, but the sound was more wry than amused. "I want to do everything at once."

"Kiss first, maybe?"

"Kiss." He nodded but didn't make a move other than that. "We can do that."

She wondered if she ought to take the reins, give him a break, but then it was as if he came to with a jerk. In one smooth movement, he swept her into his arms, pressed his body against her and brought his mouth down on hers in a hungry kiss.

It was different, kissing him this time. Knowing it was the opening act, and that she got to stay for the finale.

All his awkwardness vanished as he moved her into the apartment as if they were dancing. The heavy bass from the taproom below mirrored her heartbeat, strong and fast.

He shifted his approach to the kiss, and she managed a quick inhalation, but even as he slipped his tongue back between her lips, she put her hand on his head to keep him there. God, she didn't want to part for a second. Not when it felt this good. When she'd been so afraid of having this moment.

Why had she ever thought, even for a second, that having sex with Cam would be a bad idea? She should have known from the moment she'd caught a whiff of his scent. He smelled wonderful, and she didn't think that very often.

Now, though, she was lost in a sea of taste and touch. His hands on her back, holding her close, the way he teased her tongue into following his until she was licking the center of his upper palate.

He broke away, gasping. "Clothes," he said. "Bed." Then he stripped off his shirt in one swipe before kissing her again.

She nodded as Cam steered her to the side of the bed and climbed onto his knees, keeping her with him, mouth to mouth, until they were knee to chest on his big blue comforter. His hands moved from her back to the buttons on her blouse, which he took care of with such alacrity that she briefly wondered if he was a pianist or if he did card tricks. But when he kissed her neck as he pushed the blouse from her shoulders, she no longer cared.

"You smell so good," he said, his lips brushing her cheekbone, then making their way down toward her jaw.

She was all in favor of him showing initiative. To encourage him further, she put her hand on his chest, just above his heart.

He licked the side of her neck with his warm tongue and captured her earlobe, sucking it gently.

She gasped, getting the feel of him. He had a gorgeous chest, lean but strong. Her palm brushed a nipple and he bit her lobe, just hard enough to make her yelp.

The goose bumps that covered her arms and raced across her body were unexpected.

She hadn't even felt him unhook her bra, but she sure was aware the moment he stripped it off her and they were skin to skin, chest to chest. So different from one another.

At the thought, she lowered her hand to his fly. And why was he still wearing his jeans? The only surprise she found while cupping him was just how much of him there was to cup. And while she suspected his bottom would be hard as a rock, she knew for a fact it was true about his penis.

"Can you tell how much I want you?" he whispered, his breath warming the shell of her ear.

She went for his zipper but she wasn't coordinated enough to do the deed with one hand. Hating to part from his talented mouth, she pulled back and tackled his belt first. So efficiently, it turned out, that she pulled the whole thing clear and flung it to the floor.

The button wasn't as simple. But it didn't matter because he came to the rescue, and soon his fly was conquered and she was able to sneak her hand down, beneath the waistband of his boxers.

She felt the dampness on the backs of her knuckles seconds before she found the reason for the moisture. One finger swirled around his impossibly smooth head, making him groan like a man tortured.

Seconds later, he grabbed her wrist, pulling her hand up until she lost contact. "Why?" she said, and it sounded an awful lot like a whine.

"Miles to go," he said.

"You have a lot of willpower, Mr. Crawford."

"I'm afraid we'll finish too fast and then you'll leave."

"I'll wait until you catch your breath."

He pulled back to look at her. "Uh…"

"Kidding," she said, smiling at him. She leaned forward. Kissed the tip of his nose. "But I probably won't spend the night. I didn't bring anything with me."

"I've got an extra toothbrush. A new one. And I won't tell a living soul if you go home with no undies on. Or you can borrow a pair of my boxers. Huh." He pushed his hips against her. "That would be sexy. I'd think about it all day."

She pushed back, causing him to hiss. "Everyone will know what we did if I leave in the morning."

"Everybody already knows what we're doing."

"It's your *family*."

"So? They're not going to ask for details."

"What's your coffee situation?" she asked, bumping her hips against his, her hand still halfway down his underwear. She didn't really care about coffee, but she did want to catch her breath before the next act.

"I'm a brewmaster."

She laughed. "Touché. But seriously."

"Tell you what. If you don't love the coffee I make for you tomorrow morning, I'll run down to Starbucks and get you whatever you like."

"Promise?"

He nodded.

She kissed his nose again. Then his lips. The banter

stopped and was replaced by panting and the slick sounds of wet kisses. By the time she came back up for air, both hands were gripping his back, his jeans were halfway down his thighs, and she was aching with want.

"You have condoms?"

He nodded.

"I'm also on the pill."

"Great," he said. "But we still have too many clothes on."

"Right," she said, then maneuvered her legs over the side of the bed and stood up. Just as she was going to strip down, she looked back to find Cam still on his knees, motionless, staring at her butt, his lips parted, his pupils huge.

She decided to give him a little show. She might be crap at small talk, but she understood how to do this. Before she'd fallen into the world of wine, she'd read a lot of fiction. A lot of steamy fiction. And college had been educational in a number of ways, as well.

"Oh, God," he said, moaning as she wiggled her ass, taking her sweet time lowering her jeans. She hadn't expected this, so she hadn't worn particularly fancy panties, but he didn't seem to care.

From the sound of him, he might have actually been in pain. A quick glance over her shoulder confirmed that— yep, being that ready had to hurt, at least a little.

Once her jeans dropped, she hooked her thumbs in her plain white bikini panties and pushed them down. But before she could step out of her clothes, he grabbed her by the waist and flung her onto the bed.

She yelped again and laughed out loud. He looked like a wild man, his gritted teeth bared, kicking the last remnant of his jeans off his leg, and while she still thought he was sex on wheels, it was a sight.

Especially the bounce of his bobbing cock.

FREE Merchandise is 'in the Cards' for you!

Dear Reader,

We're giving away FREE MERCHANDISE!

Seriously, we'd like to reward you for reading this novel by giving you **FREE MERCHANDISE** worth over \$20. And no purchase is necessary!

You see the Jack of Hearts sticker above? Paste that sticker in the box on the Free Merchandise Voucher inside. Return the Voucher promptly...and we'll send you valuable Free Merchandise!

Thanks again for reading one of our novels—and enjoy your Free Merchandise with our compliments!

Pam Powers

Pam Powers

P.S. Look inside to see what Free Merchandise is **"in the cards"** for you!

W

e'd like to send you two free books like the one you are enjoying now. Your two books have a combined price of over $10, but they are yours to keep absolutely FREE! We'll even send you 2 wonderful surprise gifts. You can't lose!

REMEMBER: Your Free Merchandise, consisting of **2 Free Books** and **2 Free Gifts**, is worth over $20.00! No purchase is necessary, so please send for your Free Merchandise today.

Get TWO FREE GIFTS!

We'll also send you two wonderful FREE GIFTS (worth about $10), in addition to your 2 Free books!

Visit us at:
www.ReaderService.com

FREE MERCHANDISE VOUCHER

2 FREE
BOOKS
and
2 FREE
GIFTS

Please send my Free Merchandise, consisting of
2 Free Books and **2 Free Mystery Gifts**.
I understand that I am under no obligation to buy
anything, as explained on the back of this card.

150/350 HDL GEZC

Please Print

FIRST NAME

LAST NAME

ADDRESS

APT.#   CITY

STATE/PROV.   ZIP/POSTAL CODE

NO PURCHASE NECESSARY!

HB-714-FM13

Sidebar (rotated text): ► Detach card and mail today. No stamp needed. ▶ © 2013 HARLEQUIN ENTERPRISES LIMITED. ® and ™ are trademarks owned and used by the trademark owner and/or its licensee. Printed in the U.S.A.

She covered her face, afraid she'd spoil everything by making him self-conscious, but no, he was laughing, too.

Until he wasn't.

The shaking had stopped and he took both her wrists this time, so he could see her face. "You're gorgeous," he said. "I'm so happy you're here."

"Me, too."

"I can't even be upset that we waited. Tonight's been perfect."

"I could have done without the jitters, but it all turned out well, didn't it?"

He nodded, balanced above her as if he were about to do push-ups. "You keep surprising me," he said.

"What do you mean?"

"The conversation at dinner the first night. How amazing you were giving that speech at the banquet. Being brave enough to ask for what you really wanted. Now this."

"What's *this?* You mean wanting to sleep with you? I told you I did."

He let out a huff of breath that washed over her face. He smelled like beer and arousal. "I just… I'm really glad you picked me."

"Show me," she said.

11

CAM WAS ON FIRE. He'd imagined her naked a hundred times. Who was he kidding, five hundred at least, and he hadn't come close to the real thing. There was no part of her that didn't appeal to him, as if she'd been made to order.

He ran his tongue over the harder, uneven texture of a scar on her chest, several inches above one of the most beautiful breasts he'd ever seen. "What happened?" he asked, although she might not have understood as he was unwilling to stop licking her.

"Stabbed," she said between pants. "Accidental. I was seven."

"You were seven," he said, hating the thought, but then his attention went back to her breast.

"Oh, God," she said, the words breaking up as she gasped, her back arched.

He couldn't talk, but talking was overrated when he could suck and lick and tease and taste. It was all he could do not to just lift her legs and plunge into her, but that would end things too quickly. He wanted to wring every last gasp and moan out of her before they were through.

Okay, maybe the next time he'd stretch things out, because he didn't have a lot of time to maneuver here. Not when every brush of his cock against any part of her body nearly crippled him.

The condom. It was right on the nightstand. Too far. Way too far. But he wasn't about to let the hard, sweet nub between his lips go. He swung his hand in the approximate direction of where the condom should be. The sound of glass breaking didn't even make him blink. He just moved his hand up and down until it landed on the foil packet.

"Something fall?"

He shook his head as he switched to her other breast. "All the way over…" It was just as perfect as the first nipple, and if it wasn't for the uncomfortable pressure of his cock, he'd have hung out right where he was for a couple of days.

Her hand touched his hip and he tensed, knowing what was coming but unable to stop it.

She slipped her hand around his shaft.

He gargled. Or something. He'd never made a sound like that before. "Stop," he said, about an octave too high.

She let go instantly. "What's wrong?"

He flopped down beside her, which wasn't the most brilliant move on his part, because his dick hit his stomach a second later. "Shit," he said.

She'd turned on her side, facing him, her head propped on her hand. "What? Are you okay? Should I do something?"

Slamming his eyes shut, he shook his head. He wasn't going to be embarrassed about this. It'd happened before. When he was seventeen, but still, it was normal. "Just need a minute," he said. "To cool down."

"Oh," she said, and okay, he was a little embarrassed.

"Do you want some water or something?"

He opened his eyes, sure he'd find her laughing at him,

but she wasn't. Smiling, yeah. Also a little cocky. "You're enjoying this?"

She nodded. "Very much so."

"That's not very nice."

"I never said I was nice."

He smiled back, the acute emergency over for now, although he needed a couple more minutes. Once he was inside her, he wanted to stay as long as possible. "You're very beautiful," he said.

"Between the two of us," she said, "I think you're the better-looking one."

He dismissed that nonsense with a wave of his hand. "I wasn't finished."

"Sorry."

"And you smell great."

She giggled again. It was the best.

For now, he had to kiss her again, to run his hand down her back and feel that glorious bottom of hers. Once he got there, his thoughts fizzled away and instinct took over. Once again, she was on her back, parting her thighs at his touch so he could move up close.

Her beautiful hair was spread across his pillow, her gorgeous breasts rising and falling faster and faster. He kissed her lips then moved south. Kissing. Licking. Nibbling. Inhaling. All the way down to her adorable belly button, but her scent drew him farther yet.

Burying his nose in her trimmed V, he smoothed his palms over the astonishing softness of her inner thighs. His tongue worked its way into her cleft, the slightly sweet, pungent tang of her an aphrodisiac all its own. It made his heart beat faster to find her already swollen, her clit moist and plump between his lips.

He got comfortable and went to town, only vaguely aware of Molly's cries getting louder and her nails on his back. But he knew the second she came. Her thighs pressed against his head. A moment later, he was on his knees, sliding on the condom.

Watching him with her unfocused gaze, she said, "Now," the word carried away by her exhalation. "Please."

He lifted her legs above his hips and entered her in one long push. The sound she made was half gasp, half cry. He'd had to bite back a whimper because it was the most perfect moment in all creation. She was hot and wet and tight and all his. He stayed there for a moment, struggling to regain his breath, what little control he still had.

Then she moved. Just enough to squeeze him, and all hope was lost. He balanced himself above her so he could see her face. Her eyes. Her lips were parted with her panting, and when he started moving in and out, he could see her teeth and the way her forehead wrinkled. Hear her ragged low moan.

Her hands fisted the comforter and her legs gripped his waist. The humid heat of their breaths mingled in the space left between them. He'd felt her come. Now he wanted to see it. Feel it from the inside.

One palm spread flat on the bed, her knees separated widely enough for balance and motion, he used his free hand to change the angle of his cock as he entered her. One degree at a time. Out, then in. Holding back was going to be a problem soon, but he needed to know, to feel when he was rubbing her in exactly the right way.

There it was. More than an octave higher, her cry was accompanied by a tension that ran from her bared neck to her inner walls.

Now if he could just hold out until after she climaxed once more.

Time blurred as he forced his eyes to stay open. Watching her face, her body, the way his thrusts moved her hair, her breasts, it was like conducting his own private symphony, and he could already feel the beginning of his orgasm forming deep and low.

She began to tremble. No more sounds came out of her open mouth. It was a race to the finish, and he lost.

It was the best defeat he'd ever suffered. Every molecule in his body took part in his release. His eyes shut and his face contorted with intense pleasure. He knew she'd come only when he was able to breathe again.

A spasm squeezed his poor, exhausted cock. Next time, he'd hold on longer.

MOLLY WANTED TO tell him how amazing he was, but speaking was clearly not in the cards. Thinking was challenging, and moving was out of the question.

God, she could drink a gallon of water.

Her hand was on his chest. She wasn't sure how it had gotten there. Last she remembered, he was leaning over her, tight as a bowstring as she had another orgasm. The first in her whole life that had not only been while they were doing it, but almost at the same time as him.

She didn't even fantasize about that kind of thing. Not since Mary Louise Bennett had told her the unvarnished truth about sex when they'd been living at the group home. Molly had been ten, Mary Louise sixteen and experienced.

Molly had also carried condoms with her no matter what since that night. Frankly, she'd been more frightened than anything else, and it had only been due to Riley Finemore's charm and perseverance that she hadn't remained a virgin forever.

"I'm going to get up," Cam said, his voice startling her.

"I'm impressed."

"Necessity," he said. "But as long as I have to go, what can I bring you?"

She moved her head to the side and found him staring at her. "Water. Please. Lots."

"Got it." He smiled crookedly and sighed in resignation before hoisting himself into a sitting position. "Crap."

"What?"

"The glass breaking from before the earth moved was the water I'd so thoughtfully set out on the table."

She laughed. "You're ridiculously cute."

"I know," he said. "I swear it makes it difficult to get up some days." He scooted down the bed and made his way across her line of sight toward the kitchen. He had to swing wide, so she got to study his body. He had to be a swimmer. To get those shoulders and that waist? Definitely. Nice ass, too. Perky.

It seemed like a good time to close her eyes. Rest for a minute. "Ms. Grainger?"

She jolted awake. Cameron was there, standing, with a water bottle in his hand. Grinning at her. Shockingly, she felt a little chilly. "Hey," she said, as she awkwardly rose up on her elbows. "Thank you."

"My pleasure. If you'd like to stand up, I could pull down the comforter so you can get warm."

Being under the covers sounded great. But that would mean she really was going to spend the night. Which also meant she'd have to get up early. Really early if she wanted to catch the train before rush hour and then get back to her place to change. Damn, she'd have to wash her hair, and she had no makeup with her.

But she'd kind of promised him she'd stay.

She took the water and polished off a good half of it. He'd loosened the cap before he'd given it to her. Was he trying to make her decisions more difficult?

"No?" he asked. "Yes?"

"Ugh…" No need for him to be cold while she made up

her mind. She stood up, he threw the covers down, and she climbed back in. It was cozier when he got in, too.

He'd cleaned up the floor, gotten himself a plastic bottle for the side table... Ah, and he'd put out another condom. Optimist. Now he lay on his side, head balanced on his palm, watching her drink. "That was totally worth the wait," he said.

She swallowed. "It was. Thank you."

"The phrase *my pleasure* hasn't ever been more true."

He certainly had a way with words. "So what's this business about you saving the world?"

"Ah. First, before we continue, I want to say thanks for being so great with my annoying sisters. I don't think anyone would have guessed you were nervous at all."

"That's because you kept the spotlight just far enough away. Very kind of you."

He didn't answer. Just closed his eyes for a second. "Anyway, I'm a chemist, which you know, but I usually work for a large pharmaceutical company in Syracuse."

"I've never been there. It's not that far, is it?"

"Four and a half to five hours by train. When it's not winter."

She had enough trouble with her thirty-minute commute to Midtown. "Wow. That's pretty far."

"My team is waiting for funding from the government. Our project is focused on combating antibiotic-resistant bacteria. It's a huge operation that's really complex, because of the manner in which bacteria mutate. I mean, they were the earth's first inhabitants. They've learned a thing or two about survival."

"I've read about the problem."

"It's a tough nut to crack," he said, his voice softening as he reached over and brushed his fingers against her collarbone.

She set aside her bottle and folded the pillow so she could snuggle down and rest her head while she looked at Cam. "So that wasn't an exaggeration. You really are trying to save the world."

This time he slid his hand under the sheet and brushed the top of her breast. His touch was light, the motion repetitive. It felt nice.

"Not really," he said. "Trying to make a difference, yeah. But it's just as likely I'll work on this project for the rest of my life and we won't find the magic bullet."

"It takes a special kind of person to make a commitment like that without knowing the ultimate outcome."

"I don't think anyone ever really knows the outcome. I may get so fed up with the internal politics of big pharma, I'll quit and come back here and make beer until I'm old and gray. It wouldn't be a bad life."

"I suppose not," she said. "But I think the world already has a lot of talented brewmasters."

The petting stopped, although his hand remained on her. "Let me ask you something. Why did it make a difference?"

"Hmm?"

He seemed to approve of the folded-pillow technique and did the same to his own so they were very close, eye to eye, resting on their sides, before he caressed her again. "When you found out I'm only here for a few months. Why did that change your mind?"

She sighed. "In my experience, sex complicates everything. I'm not in a position to let everything get complicated."

"Everything?"

"I've got a great deal riding on the next five years. I have every intention of becoming an important figure in the wine world. Phillip and Simone have been training me since I was sixteen. I'm good at what I do, but with the internet, the field has really opened up. You can't just be good and get anywhere. You have to be spectacularly good, and it's not enough to be good at only judging wine. A lot of my work is writing, and that isn't nearly as natural to me as being a sommelier. But the more I'm published, the more I'll become known. Since writing is difficult for me, having my attention splintered could really get in the way of my dreams."

"Okay, that makes sense. But we're having sex, and I was hoping this wasn't a one-off."

"No, I'd like to do it again. Knowing you're leaving means I won't let my libido turn my brain to mush." She carefully kept her eyes even with his. "So we're good."

His gaze shifted for the first time since he'd come back with her water, and his hand retreated. She wanted it back. There was no reason for him to be hurt. This wasn't really new information. "I understand," he said, but she didn't think he was telling the truth.

"There was a reason you had 'one-night stand' on your trading card. You didn't want to get involved. I'd assumed you were commitment-phobic, but after seeing you with your family, I think you're the opposite."

"Really?"

She nodded. "I think you want a wife and a family, but you want them close. It wouldn't do to fall for someone who lives in Brooklyn when you're moving to Syracuse."

His half smile and slow blink showed her she'd been right.

"I figure," she said, touching his arm, "that we've got the best of both worlds. Neither of us can get involved, and yet we're smoking hot in bed, and outside of bed we've found a great quid pro quo solution to some pressing problems. This four-month stand can be four pretty sweet months."

"Except for the fact that you have the craziest schedule ever."

"There is that, but just because I've had to give up movies and vacations and sleep doesn't mean I have to be a nun. It's all a matter of keeping my eye on the prize and utilizing my time well."

He smiled. The shadow that had darkened his face vanished, and it wasn't a trick of the light. "I like the way you think."

Moving closer to him, she was able to run her hand down his back, all the way to the little dimples above his butt. "Well, then you won't be too disappointed when I tell you I've got to go home tonight."

"The hell I won't." He put his palm on her cheek, and she couldn't hold back from nuzzling him. "I promised you coffee."

"I know. But in order to get to work on time tomorrow, I'd have to wake up around four-thirty. I can get along without much sleep, but I can't start the day off like that."

"No, I remember. Fridays are tough." He leaned in for a kiss.

It would have been simple, staying. But dangerous.

It might be a four-month stand, but there was no need to take unnecessary risks. It was enough that she liked him enormously. He was a gift, and she'd do whatever she needed to in order to keep the status quo.

On the other hand, it wouldn't kill her to kiss him for a little bit longer.

12

"SLEEP WELL." Cam stood at her door, one step from leaving. They'd already kissed goodbye, and yet he couldn't help but hope she would ask him to stay.

"You, too," she said. "Thanks for seeing me home."

The door closed. He walked away, wishing…for what? The whole reason she'd come back to her place was to get as much sleep as she could, and having someone new in her bed wasn't exactly conducive to crashing fast and hard. Especially when one of them would absolutely have an erection.

He banged on the door of the elevator. It hurt.

Cam closed his eyes as he slowly descended to the ground floor. There was no reason for him to be upset, so WTF? She hadn't changed her mind about spending the night because she didn't like him anymore. Their last kiss had proved that. Hell, the whole ride home they'd sat so close together, neutrons couldn't have squeezed between them. They'd already made plans about talking tomorrow…later today. She'd been great with his family and the sex had been…

Of course it had felt like the best sex he'd ever had. He'd been wanting it since that first night and it had been postponed. Twice.

A blast of hot, humid air swept over him as he walked to the street, already getting a sweat on. By the time he got home and showered, it would be late. Molly wasn't the only one who had a busy day tomorrow.

The annual Albany Charity Beer Fest was coming up in a couple of weeks, and he was entering six of their new seasonal beers. Then there was the Hop Fest and Hudson River Fest. The Four Sisters needed some blue ribbons. It had been too long between victories, and although the summer had been good to the bar so far, they needed to be busy year-round. Which meant he had to work on the fall and winter seasonal brews so that the recipes would be in place when he left. Once the Syracuse team was up and running, he'd be back to having regular vacations, not eight to ten months at his disposal.

What The Four Sisters needed was another brewmaster, but Gordon was a stubborn bastard. He liked everything to stay the way it always had. Which was a damn shame, because he needed to move forward with his life.

There were plenty of women who'd give their eyeteeth to hook up with Gordon Crawford, but no one could replace his Jewel. Twenty-eight years was a long time to hold on to the past. Not that Gordon had been a monk all this time, but he'd never contemplated a serious relationship.

As far as Cam was concerned, his sisters would be doing everyone a favor if they focused on setting their dad up with a keeper, not him. His old man had found the perfect chemistry once. It was possible he could find it again. Maybe.

The whole family was more stubborn than smart.

He sighed as he headed down the steps of the subway station to catch his ride home. At least he knew he'd be seeing Molly a week from Saturday.

MOLLY STARED AT her calendar, forcing herself to really look
at what the past four days had been like. It had been bad
enough that she'd slept through her alarm Friday morning, which had thrown off her rhythm the whole day, but
that she'd spent the afternoon daydreaming like a twelve-
year-old girl was ridiculous. She'd lost her footing in two
important meetings, she'd nearly broken her neck at the
gym because her thoughts had been on Cam instead of
what she was doing, and most appallingly, she'd missed
properly identifying the origin of a Shiraz during the blind
tasting at the largest wine shop in Manhattan.

To say she'd been humiliated was an understatement,
but she'd been humiliated before and lived through it. The
real problem was still not being able to put Cameron in
the box.

Admittedly, the past two days had been better. While
she hadn't succeeded in forgetting about Cam completely,
she'd regained her focus at work, even during long hours
spent writing columns and grading papers.

Yesterday, though, things had once again deteriorated.
She doubted anyone she'd spoken with had noticed a thing,
but that didn't mean she wasn't in serious trouble.

She and Cam were supposed to have talked on the phone
Sunday night. She'd penciled him in for an hour at ten.
But two minutes after the hour, her buzzer had rung. He'd
promised he'd stay only for the allotted time, and it could
have worked, considering how quickly they'd gotten naked.
But she hadn't set an alarm.

One hour had become two. They'd both gotten carried
away. She'd been so ready, and he'd been so hard, she
hadn't been able to resist taking him in her mouth. She'd
always liked doing that, and he'd been ecstatic. Remem-
bering the sounds she'd wrested from him made her shiver
even now.

But he'd stopped her before he finished, flipped her onto her back and returned the favor. Damn but he wasn't just a great brewmaster—he was an expert with his tongue and fingers, as well.

She'd come so hard, she nearly clipped him in the jaw. Cam had surprised her yet again by helping her to her hands and knees. He was tall enough that he lay over her back as he plunged inside her, hands on her waist to help her keep still. Then the devil had started whispering in her ear.

Soft, hot, naughty things. A list of all the ways he wanted to ravish her. His voice alone made her clench her muscles so hard, she'd felt it in the morning, and then when his right hand had moved down to her clit, she'd shattered. Memories of his touch, his voice, the scent of sex and the sound of their gasps were on a repeating loop in her head.

Somehow, he'd gathered himself together enough to dress and head home.

She'd been useless and had gotten no more work done.

Naturally, she'd been tired Monday morning, and she hadn't been able to get back in her groove. Not with the massive sex hangover. She hadn't even known that was a thing. Unfortunately, there didn't seem to be a cure.

Something had to be done, and she'd come to the conclusion that the problem was the novelty of being together. The lag between sexual encounters had been too wide. The obvious answer was to have sex more often. Become accustomed to each other. Their arrangement needed to work for months to come and she was determined to fit Cam into her schedule, even if it meant giving up almost everything else that wasn't work or sleep.

All things became more normal with time, even the most exciting moments, if they were repeated often enough.

They'd discuss her plan on Saturday. After the event. Before sex.

Okay, maybe right after.

CAMERON SIPPED HIS excellent Merlot as he watched Molly do her thing. The event was being held at the Hudson Square Wine Festival, at the City Winery in Soho. It was a cavernous music hall, wine bar, restaurant and subterranean winery that suited him to a T. He'd have liked to have spent more time talking to the vintners, but he was there for Molly.

Good thing, too, because there had been lots of milling about between tastings where he was able to smooth her way. There was even a brilliant workshop where amateur enologists were given the chance to produce their own vintage, from picking the grapes to creating their own blend and even designing a label. He could easily imagine doing that at The Four Sisters—with beer, of course—but it would take a great deal of time, effort and money to put it together well. Which he wouldn't be around to do.

So he stood guard, as relaxed in his slacks and sport jacket as Molly appeared in her slinky beige dress that showed off her figure and made it difficult not to steal her away.

Now she and four other wine experts were tasting a number of wines, doing their swirls and sniffs and spits and notes, and it was all accompanied by a live jazz band on the stage. The place was packed, even with the thousand-dollar-per-person price tag.

He found it impossible to look at anything but Molly. Christ, he'd missed her. Even though they'd spoken on the phone daily, it hadn't been enough. Every night the thought of her in his bed and his arms played like a loop in his head. Jacking off eased the pressure, but it was like drinking ginger beer when he was craving strong Belgian ale.

All he had to do was hang tough until after dinner. So he sipped his wine until it was her turn to talk about the wines she'd tasted, and then he couldn't do a damn thing but hold his breath and watch her make her points with eloquence and tact using a combination of scientific observations and poetics. She had the crowd in the palm of her hand. One wine she'd called a full-bodied Marilyn Monroe, which made people laugh.

Finally they made their way to her apartment, both a little tipsy and high on the success of the evening. He felt as if he were walking on a cloud. Maybe it was just that he got to kiss her. And that she was so happy.

The only things that had changed in her studio since the last time he'd been there were the information on the whiteboard and the items on her desk.

Molly put her purse down, slipped out of her heels, then came right up close to him, her arms sliding around his waist. "Before we go any further," she said, "I was wondering if you'd care to spend the night."

"Hmm. Let me think for a minute."

"You ought to. Tomorrow may be Sunday, but I still have to get up early."

"Why on earth would you do that?"

"Sunday mornings are for writing. If I sleep too late, I tend to let myself off the hook, and I pay for that indulgence. Which means while I do want you here, we'll need to be…"

"Do not say 'quick,'" he pleaded. "Please. Anything but quick."

"On task," she replied, smiling.

"Okay, I should've qualified that better."

She leaned into him. "And in the morning, you're welcome to shower in the kitchen, but then it'll be coffee to go, and I kick you out."

"Wow, you are one tough negotiator."

She inhaled, and it made her breasts press against his chest. He wanted to take off his jacket, but he wouldn't disturb her for anything. "I have to be. It's this or nothing, I'm afraid. The only way to make this work is to stick to the schedule. I'd actually like to see you more often, but sticking to the rules would need to be nonnegotiable."

"I'm very in favor of this plan. In fact, this is a prize-winning plan that should be celebrated. Soon."

"Then I suggest you do whatever it is you need to do before we begin, and I'll do the same."

He made a show of raising his arm. "Should we synchronize our watches?"

She nipped his chin. "Just hurry. I've been thinking about this for too long."

One quick but passionate kiss later, he was in the bathroom, brushing his teeth. He'd come prepared tonight with condoms, a travel toothbrush and the hope that they'd come back to her place. He'd never dreamed of such a great outcome.

She took his place, and as he was taking off his clothes, he saw there were two plastic water bottles on either side of her bed.

Before he got completely naked, he folded down the covers and left them on the floor. He wanted nothing to get in the way of this delicate operation. His intention was to give her as much pleasure as possible and to reinforce her decision to do this every chance they could grab.

MOLLY'S BACK ARCHED so high, she thought she might sprain something. It was worth it, though, as she was electrified by an orgasm that rushed through her body like a wave.

Her hands were in his hair, although she wasn't moving him away or keeping him in place because she couldn't decide what she wanted. The pleasure was so close to being too much, but stopping was out of the question.

She didn't have much say, it turned out, because he pulled back, and even though she thought she'd ripped out some of his hair, he didn't seem to mind. Instead, he lifted her legs and put them not on his hips, which she was expecting, but on his shoulders, and holy cow, how glad was she to have been taking yoga?

Cruelly, he made her wait while he put on the condom, but seconds later, he thrust inside her so hard, so deep, she might have just woken not only the neighbors in her building, but the ones across the alley.

"Good gah," she said, completely aware *gah* wasn't a word and not caring at all. In fact, all she could manage from that point on were a series of *ah, ah, ah*s as she pulled the fitted sheet free from the mattress.

She tried so, so hard to watch his face in its most feral state, his teeth bared, his skin flushed red and his breath exploding with each furious exhalation.

Time got all messed up because she was coming again and he was leaning way over her. One leg was on the bed, one still on his shoulder, and he wasn't moving at all. But he was groaning so loudly, the next step was probably a visit by the police.

When she came back to her senses, he was at her side. They were plastered together by their sticky flesh, panting with no rhythm at all, and she felt sure she'd lost about a gazillion brain cells, because she couldn't put two thoughts together.

Through some miracle she couldn't explain, a bottle of cold water ended up in her hand. Again, time had hopped like a bunny, because suddenly she could breathe like a normal human and the air coming from her stupid window unit was actually giving her goose bumps.

"That," she said, considering the effort it would take to rise up on her elbow to drink, "was incredible."

A grunt from next to her signaled Cam's agreement.

She finally marshaled all her energy and rose up far enough to drink, and she nearly polished off all sixteen ounces.

Finally, she looked at Cam. And laughed out loud at not only his hair, which was hilariously sticking out as if he'd been electrocuted, but his immensely satisfied grin.

"Thirty-two minutes," he said.

"Wow."

He nodded. "Damn, I'm good."

"I didn't think men were supposed to be pleased about being fast."

"Hey. You're the one who made the rules."

"And you took that as a challenge, I assume."

"Damn straight. No half measures from this guy. Not for you."

She leaned over and kissed him. "Thank you."

"Do you have to go to sleep right this second?"

She shook her head. "Not right this second."

"Good." He stood up, nearly bumping into the wall in his rush. Instead of going straight to the bathroom, he gathered up the covers and put them back on the bed. Not very neatly, but it was still a nice example of modern-day chivalry.

Soon enough, she'd finished her turn in the bathroom, turned off the lights and snuggled close to him under the covers. "Question."

"Shoot."

"For someone who isn't supposed to be athletic, you're in damn fine shape."

"Swimming. I started in college."

"I knew it," she said.

"How?"

"I'm a genius."

"It's the shoulders," he said. "Am I right?"

"I guess you're a genius, too."

"My nosy sisters have no idea I swim competitively. And I win, often. Makes me feel superior when they act like they know everything." Cam looked so adorably smug, it made her laugh. "Hey, how come you call your folks Phillip and Simone?"

"Hello, non sequitur," she said, not sure why her chest had tightened. Her relationship to them was no secret. "What brought that on?"

"Dad asked if you'd like to bring them over for dinner sometime, and I realized I didn't know much about them."

"They're not my parents." There wasn't any specific reason she hadn't told him about being a foster kid, but then again, he had a family and there were so many ideas and stereotypes about growing up in the system.

"Wait, those are the people you referred to as your mentors, right?"

She nodded. "They were my foster family when I was fifteen. I lived with them for three years, until I went away to college."

He squeezed her a little tighter. "You grew up in foster care?"

She nodded and looked at him in the very dim light. She wasn't sure what his expression was, not precisely. She hoped like hell it didn't look like pity. "Yep."

"That doesn't sound like much fun."

"I don't recommend it. But I'm luckier than a lot of kids. I was in a really good group home when I was young. No horror stories, other than not being adopted."

"That makes no sense to me. You're adorable now. I can only imagine you as a little girl."

She bumped her head to his. "I was shy. I mean really, really shy. The kind that was off-putting to potential parents. When I said I wasn't picked, that's not accurate. I never stuck. Until Simone and Phillip came along."

"They weren't at the banquet."

For the first time in the conversation, she truly felt uncomfortable. She wanted to explain how busy they were, how much they were needed at the vineyard this time of year. Instead, she said, "They live in France. They moved shortly after I left for college in Sonoma. We keep in touch."

"Too bad they couldn't have been there, though."

She shrugged and yawned, although she'd hadn't needed to.

He kissed her forehead. "Okay, sleepyhead. You have your alarm set?"

"Uh-huh. You won't be so chipper when it rings."

"I can't wait to wake up next to you," he said, his lips close to her ear. "Anytime."

Well, she thought as she moved her head to get settled on her pillow instead of his shoulder. This might not have worked out quite the way she'd hoped. The fact that she would wake up to Cam made her want to fall asleep instantly and at the same time not sleep at all so she wouldn't miss a second. So yeah, he was still a distraction.

But she'd deal with that tomorrow. Tonight she would enjoy being in this happy place until she fell asleep.

13

ON FRIDAY NIGHT the pub was standing room only. Luckily, Cam wasn't needed up front, so he stayed in the back working on Molly's IPA. It was coming along just fine. Over the past few days, Cam had ended up drinking an entire bottle of Cabernet Sauvignon trying to work out everything he could about the flavor, the astringency, the mouthfeel of the noble grapes and the particular blend of the vintner. Nothing more to tell now, not until the fermentation was complete. Of course, it wouldn't taste like wine, but that wasn't the point.

He wanted to surprise her. To give her something only he could. No one ever said chemists didn't have big egos.

But he needed to shift his energy over to the fall brews, despite the fact that it was past eight o'clock and he hadn't eaten any dinner. The fall beers were in different stages, two having been failures, which was disappointing. They'd sounded good on paper, but there'd been a chalky aftertaste in one, and he had a feeling the second ale would be better with wheat than barley, so that was next on his agenda.

As he went to the malting kiln for the final roast, he thought about Molly's schedule. As hard as they'd tried to meet since last Saturday night, it hadn't worked out.

He still felt bad about her falling asleep in the middle of phone sex Tuesday. His fault. He'd heard the exhaustion in her voice. Then on Wednesday, when she'd had some free time, he'd been caught up in a drama at the bar. There'd been a fight and the police had been involved. By the time things were resolved, she'd gone to bed.

Tonight she was teaching a wine class and wouldn't be home for another hour or so. He'd wait to give her a call, but not too long. If he caught her in transit, maybe he could convince her to meet him for a drink. Not at the pub—somewhere else, where they didn't know anyone. Good Lord, he missed her.

The lonely week had given him time to think about how he still knew so little about her. Maybe it wasn't his business, but she seemed reluctant to open up much about her past. More often than not, she'd turn his questions around. Molly knew a hell of a lot about his childhood. But even though he'd told her he'd lost his mother when he was five, she'd never asked what had happened, and he'd never volunteered the information. He still wasn't sure why.

The scent of the toasted wheat was fantastic, but it would be even better when he added the chocolate malt. First he tasted a bit of the wheat, making sure that the flavor was what he had in mind. Closing his eyes so he could focus completely, he let his senses lead the way through the process, making sure he used all the parts of his tongue and breathed deeply to catch all the subtlety he could.

He heard a sniffle before he looked and saw that it was Emmy, standing not two feet away from him, her eyes red rimmed and damp. "What? What's happened?"

"Men are jerks," she said.

"Thanks for the vote of confidence. What have we done now?"

"The new guy sucked. And I spent a lot of money on this dress."

It wasn't like Emmy to be so…girlie. He had to admit, she did look pretty in her pale blue halter dress, although he wasn't sure about the shoes. The heels added at least five inches to her six-foot frame. Maybe she'd intimidated her new guy and he'd made a run for it. "What did he do?"

She tossed her purse on top of one of the closed barrels of malt then leaned against a post, her arms crossed over her chest. "He was supposed to take me out to dinner. His trading card said his favorite restaurant was Babbo, that *Iron Chef* guy's restaurant, so when Ronny said he wanted to surprise me, I expected, you know, Babbo."

"Uh-oh."

"Hey," she said, pointing at Cam. "You know me. I'm not all about the money, so it wasn't that I wanted him to spend beaucoup bucks."

"I do know that. Where did he take you?"

"Chili's. I mean, I like Chili's. Chili's is great. But it's not where you take someone you want to impress. Not on a first date. We had to wait in line for, like, twenty minutes. And then he kept ordering margaritas, and by the time we were ready to go, he was drunk and handsy, and he kept trying to stick his tongue down my throat."

"Okay, I see your point about him being a jerk, although I don't think he necessarily speaks for the entire gender."

"I was looking forward to him. We'd had a great conversation on the phone. We had so much in common. He loves basketball and beer, and he's from a big family, too, and he lives in Brooklyn, so it isn't too far. I don't know why I keep trying. It's so much easier for you guys. Hell, you go out on one date with Molly and it's true love. You're probably already planning the wedding."

"It's not like that. I'm sorry you're unhappy, though. I know it takes a lot to find the right person. I always say—"

"I swear to God, if you say one word about chemistry, I'm going to kick you into next year."

He held up his hands. She hadn't beaten him up since he was a kid, but he wasn't about to take any chances. "Come on," he said. "Let me buy you a beer. You can tell me all about it."

"You're working."

He shrugged. "It's late. Nothing that can't wait."

Emmy sniffed again. "I didn't even get dessert."

"One dessert, coming up." He put his arm around her and she rested her head on his shoulder.

"I'm so glad you're not that guy. You were damn lucky to be raised by us women. No wonder Molly likes you so much."

"Uh-oh. You've said something nice about me. He really must have been a jerk."

"Shut up, you little twerp. You had dinner yet?"

"Nope."

His cell phone rang. He hoped it was Molly, but he hesitated.

"Go ahead. Answer," Emmy told him. "It might be Molly. Anyway, I don't need you to be there when I eat a whole cheesecake."

He knew she wasn't kidding and grabbed his phone. "How come you're not in class?"

"I let them go half an hour early."

"What's wrong?"

"You, that's what. My whole plan depended on seeing you more, not less."

"I'm right with you. Where are you now?"

"I'm almost at Queens Boulevard. I can be at your place in ten."

"I'll meet you at the station."

"No, that's okay. Just get the water ready and take off whatever you're wearing. I want you ready."

"I'm already ready," he said.

"Gotta go. We're coming to a stop."

Cam noticed he was alone. Emmy must have left to get her cheesecake. As quickly as he could walk with his burgeoning erection, he made it outside and up the staircase. He hadn't even made his bed this morning, and there were clothes on the floor, so he shoved those in his closet and threw the covers to the floor.

He'd barely stepped out of his jeans and boxers when she opened his door.

Man, she was dressed in her work clothes. Sharp black slacks, crisp white blouse with the top two buttons undone…

"I must say, this was a great decision on my part."

He nodded as he walked toward her.

"I like it when you're already naked," she said, putting her purse and briefcase away on the counter behind her without even looking. "Sexy."

He stopped just shy of being able to touch her, and instead touched himself. A long slow pull on his now-hard penis. She shivered. "Just so you know, I've already set my watch. We have one hour and ten minutes. Then I'm leaving. Got it?"

He blinked. "An hour and ten? Come on, woman. Quit staring at me and get your clothes off."

She smiled. They both tackled the job and in short order they were on the bed, the light was off and she was helping him put on his condom. "What, no foreplay?" he asked. "I like foreplay."

"As do I, but I like cuddling, too. If you wouldn't mind."

He cupped her cheek. "Cuddling it is."

"After," she said, moving in close. When she kissed him, it was fast and deep.

Cam was nothing if not willing to play along. While he liked the sensuality of a slow seduction, there was a lot to say about down and dirty. He still made sure she was ready for him and was rewarded with a low moan and a quick thrust of her hips.

Seconds before he was going to lay her down, she stopped him. "I think tonight we'll go cowboy-style."

"You really did like me being naked for you."

Her grin was wicked. "Someone's got to make sure we wrap this up in time."

He flopped down on his back and threw his arms out wide. "I'm yours. Any way you want me."

She mounted him in one quick move then rode him like Annie Oakley.

Not only did she get her cuddle, they walked with their arms around each other to the station, both of them grinning like idiots the whole time.

SHE'D MEANT TO say Gewürztraminer. The interview had been about wines from the Alsace region of France. To the best of Molly's recollection, it was only after the fourth mention of Grüner Veltliner, a completely different white from Austria, that the interviewer from *Food & Wine* magazine had corrected her. Nicely. With barely a hint of pity.

It was the first time she'd been the interviewee in an article asking for expert opinions, a direct result of her win at the International Wine Writers Association.

An hour later the humiliation of her faux pas was still fresh and resting heavily in her gut, but the pain of what she had to do next lay in her heart. Cameron had to go.

The subway rocked as it took a curve, but she found his trading card easily tucked away in her purse. He was so much more than handsome now. His photo hadn't been able to catch the way his eyes narrowed seconds before he said something he hoped would make her laugh. How endearing his lopsided smile was. The way, when he looked at her, he saw so much more than she could see in herself.

Maybe she wouldn't put the card back into the pile. Not that she'd hold on to it forever. That would be selfish and wrong. But he'd never asked her to put his card back into circulation, so maybe she could keep it for now, just to be sure.

Sure of what, though? That she really couldn't see him again? Wasn't the interview proof enough?

She'd already sacrificed so much for her career and her future, letting go of Cam shouldn't be that hard. They both understood they weren't anything but temporary. She was always supposed to have been his pretend girlfriend. Except the pretend part had become blurred, at least for her. So, yes, this was the right thing to do. Absolutely.

So why was it tearing her up inside? Why hadn't she been able to get a full breath since she'd made her decision?

She held on to his card the whole way to St. Marks, even though she could only snatch looks at it when they hit the stops before hers. She knew one thing for certain: he'd lied about his favorite restaurant. Not that he'd admitted it. But the way he'd waxed rhapsodic about cheeseburgers and the pulled pork at The Four Sisters? Prune was a very fine restaurant, but they served things like fried sweetbreads and roasted marrow bones.

As for the rest of the card…the answers were only half-truths.

He didn't really want a one-night stand. While he was in Queens, yes, but Cameron was a man destined for a wife and family. No question. And he'd want a wife who was there for him and the kids. Not that he wouldn't want her to have a job, but he'd pick someone who had only a job, not a career.

The death of his mother at such a young age probably meant he'd want a stay-at-home mom for his children. God, Cam's ideal life consisted of a meaningful job in Syracuse, with a house and a dog and room in the basement to experiment with his home brews. He'd want a lot of kids, too. Not that he'd said as much, but she knew.

No matter how she tried to make herself fit into that picture, she couldn't. She'd never be that wife in that life. *Having* a family of her own? What did she know about that?

Thirty minutes later, she almost walked past the church and had to backpedal a few steps before she made her way down to the basement. The room was once again crowded, filled with laughter and the kind of small talk that gave her hives. This time things were different, though. She tried to imagine each woman there as a potential partner for Cam, but she had to stop. Doing so made her feel sick.

So she found an unobtrusive spot by the radiator, leaned against the wall and closed her eyes.

God, she had to put his card back, didn't she? There was no way she could do anything else. It hurt like the devil, but then, it would, wouldn't it? She liked him. More than she'd liked any man before. Still, the end was inevitable, if it happened today or in three or four months.

She'd find another card. Maybe not someone as great as Cam, but that was a good thing, because then it really would be an advantage to stick to the one-night stand. She didn't even care about the back of the card this time. Screw wanting someone who shared a common interest. The less talking, the better. All she wanted was someone who was hot. Who looked as if he'd know what to do between the sheets.

Luckily, no one bothered her in her little corner. She

hadn't made any friends; that wasn't the point. Donna wasn't there today because she was still seeing Wayne. Not even Emmy was—

Molly's breath caught and she scanned the room. God. How could she have forgotten about Cam's sister? More proof that she'd lost control and was sinking fast. Wrapped up in her humiliation, she'd left the interview and headed straight to the meeting without thinking it through. Emmy couldn't catch her returning Cam's card.

Molly started to relax. Emmy was tall and not easily missed.

The woman with this month's batch of cards came into the room. The box was left out for anyone to return cards, and even though Molly's grip tightened on Cam's card, she knew what she had to do.

This was her reality. Her life. She'd said Grüner Veltliner. She hadn't been thinking of Cameron that particular second; in fact, she'd been concentrating on the interview with all her might. But she'd never made a mistake like that before. Not when it was so important.

If that article came out with her mistake in it… She couldn't bear to think about what Phillip would say. He and Simone would be so ashamed.

Molly walked over to the tables and forced herself to release the card before she could change her mind. It felt as if she were stabbing a knife into her own heart. She watched as the cards were shaken, moved, and his picture submerged slowly into the pile.

Then the box was lifted high, shaken again, and the contents were dumped so that anyone could reach in and find it. Take him.

The last thing she wanted was someone else's card. But she couldn't pay attention to her overemotional whining. This was the right move. Replacing Cam as quickly as possible was what she had to do if she wanted to get her career back on track. There was someone. Blond hair, nice smile, green eyes. She plucked the card from the table and stepped back, letting other women have their chance.

"Molly, hey."

Molly nearly jumped out of her skin at Emmy's voice behind her. She turned to find Cam's sister staring at the trading card in Molly's hand.

"It's for a friend. She's going to be late, but she asked me to find someone her type, and—" she lifted the card, read the back "—Adam is perfect."

"Oh, man. I thought… Well, I won't tell you what I thought. So you're here for…"

"Susan." Molly had no idea if there was a Susan in the group, but she'd already dug herself a pit of lies, so what was one more? "She's only been here a few times."

"I wish I was here for a friend." Emmy looked at the card she had in her hand. "This guy's bottom line is that he's ready to settle down. Which sounds great because I am, too. But his passion is extreme sports. It doesn't sound promising, does it?"

Molly felt guiltier by the second. "No. It doesn't. A man who's ready to settle down wouldn't willingly put himself into dangerous situations. Is he a fireman or a soldier or something?"

Emmy nodded. "Close enough. He's a cop." She shook her head as she tossed the card back in the pile. "I will never admit this to my brother, but I swear he's the real deal. If I could find a man like him…"

Molly had a hard time finding an appropriate expression. She ended up smiling. "He's really something," she said. "It'll be hard to say goodbye when he goes back to Syracuse."

"Who says you'll have to say goodbye?"

"My work is here." Molly wanted to recall her words the second she'd said them. It could ruin everything for Cam if his family thought she wouldn't go with him. Although that wouldn't be a consideration for long. He'd have to tell them at some point that their relationship had ended. "On the other hand," she said, "there are more important things than work, right?"

Emmy nodded. "I haven't seen him this happy in a long time. He's so focused on his work, he forgets that he has needs, too. And not just the obvious ones. He'll be such a good dad and husband."

"You going to go back in? Search for someone else's card?"

"Nope." Emmy hoisted her purse strap over her shoulder. "I'm gonna sit this round out. You want to get a cup of coffee or something?"

"Thanks, but I'm going to take one more look through to see if there's anyone who can beat out Adam."

"Okay. See you soon."

Molly nodded, grinning as if she meant it, until Emmy was out of the room, and then she dived back into the pile of cards, desperate to find Cameron's. What an idiot she'd been to toss him back. Anyone could see that what Emmy had said about him was true. Any woman who was the least bit interested in a relationship would be all over him. Just because she wasn't one of them didn't mean she wanted him to fall in love while he was still here. She didn't know anyone in this group outside of Donna. They could be horrible people.

It might not be the right thing to do, but she wasn't willing to give him back until she had to.

Unfortunately, after going through the pile of cards three times, she had to face the truth. Cameron's card was gone. She thought about barricading the door until she got it back, but so many people had left. How could it hurt this much when she and Cam had no future? He deserved to find the right woman. And she needed to back off until she got him out of her system. Yet all she could think of was how he'd held her Friday night. How he'd run his hands through her hair and made all her worries vanish.

What had she done?

14

CAM HAD JUST gotten into bed after a hell of a long day. It was past two and he wanted nothing more than to crash. He'd left a message for Molly, telling her he'd be closing the bar and that she could call whenever it was convenient if she had time, but he hoped she was sleeping.

As he reached for his bedside light, his cell phone rang and he took it out of the charger. "Molly. What are you doing up so late on a Wednesday night?"

"Technically that would be early on a Thursday morning."

"Details, details." He turned off the lamp anyway, then lay back on his pillow, not half so tired anymore. "I'm glad you called."

"I've been thinking about you," she said.

Something didn't sit right. Between her first sentence and her second, her voice had changed. "That's good, because I think about you a lot."

"During work?"

"Are you kidding? I can't keep my mind off you. I'm a hormonal sixteen-year-old all over again."

She laughed, but nope. There was something going on. "Molly, you okay?"

"Of course," she said, then sighed. "I had a stressful day. Which is one of the reasons I wanted to talk to you."

Cam sat up and turned the light back on. "What happened?"

There was a long pause where he could hear her breathing, but nothing more. It made him anxious, but he didn't want to rush her.

"I made a mistake," she said, finally. "Something that sounded like the right thing, but I don't think it is."

"Can you tell me about it?"

Another pause, but this time her breath was shaky. Was she crying? "Honey?" he said, lowering his voice, wishing he could see her.

"I'd planned to, but now I don't think I can," she said. "Not yet."

Not yet? "That's fine." His chest tightening, he felt helpless but he knew not to push. "Is there anything I can do?"

"Talk to me?"

"About?"

"I don't know." Molly sounded so lost, it sliced through him. "Your mom?"

That startled him. Had something happened to Simone? It was such an odd request, but then, growing up without a mother was something else they had in common. "I don't remember her much," he said. Maybe she'd tried to look for her parents and found out something bad? But he wouldn't ask. She'd tell him when she was ready. "I was only five when she died, and even though we had pictures of her and some home movies and stuff, it was like seeing someone in the role of Mom, you know? Like when you buy a picture frame and there's this happy couple already in it. So I used to make up stories about her. I knew her real history from my dad, but my versions were better. For a year I'd convinced myself that she was working undercover. That she'd come back one day, surprise us all. And my dad would stop being sad.

"I'm not sure about your circumstances, how you ended up in the foster system, but I assumed…" He sucked in a breath, wishing he'd thought for a minute before he'd started talking. "I'd assumed you probably did that, too. Made up stories about your mom."

"I did," she said, her tone lighter, but still not *Molly*. "I made up stories all the time. I was really young when I was abandoned. No one has any idea who my parents were. I was just a little kid left at a YMCA in Midtown. Like in the movies."

"Damn," he said. "That's rough."

"No, I was okay. Lucky. It only got hard when I was old enough to realize I wasn't wanted. That felt personal."

"So you used to think they'd come back and get you?"

"Constantly. It was never their fault. Something terrible had happened. Mostly, when I was really little I thought they'd been carried away by a tornado like Dorothy in *The Wizard of Oz*. Then later it was Voldemort who had them. I think Harry Potter helped more than anything else ever could have. I used to draw a *Z* on my forehead. When I was fifteen, I tried to have it tattooed. But the artist wouldn't do it without permission."

"I imagine you're pretty grateful that didn't happen."

"Some days I wish I had."

Cam winced. "Was today like that?"

Her bitter laugh told him the answer even before she said, "I don't deserve that mark today. I doubt I ever did."

"I wish you were here so I could look you in the eyes and tell you that's not true. You're remarkable. In so many ways. Whatever it is you did, I know there had to be a reason. It'll all work out. I promise."

"Oh, Cam…don't say that." She let out a shaky breath.

"You know what? I've kept us both up too long. I'll talk to you later, okay?"

"Molly—"

She'd already disconnected. Cam got up. He wasn't tired any longer, and he thought about getting dressed, going over to her place. But for all he knew, he'd just make things worse. Besides, that was what a boyfriend would do.

A glass of water was a crappy thing to drink when the issue was Molly and the answer unclear, but it was too late for alcohol. Except for the fact that they were now having sex, her goals for their relationship hadn't changed at all. There was exactly one thing she wanted them to be: convenient. That was all. He'd already stepped into the murky water of liking her too much. To rush to her side would be crossing a line. It hardly mattered that he didn't know where the line was.

MOLLY WOKE UP groggy and miserable after taking an over-the-counter sleep aid shortly after hanging up with Cam. But at least she'd gotten four hours of sleep. It wasn't enough. Unfortunately, the four hours hardly made a dent in her sleep deprivation. Her fault for not coming clean about the trading card.

To get out of bed and go to breakfast with Donna, or to call with an excuse? That was the question. If it were simply a social engagement she wouldn't have hesitated to cancel, but Donna was also her editor and they had business to discuss. Afterward, she had to finish writing a proposal for a new radio show, then late this afternoon, Molly had to attend a meeting at WNYU, which she simply couldn't miss.

She forced herself to get up. She made her coffee extra strong. Even her shower didn't help much, and by the time she got to Penelope in Midtown East, Donna had already ordered her eggs Benedict, which was Molly's favorite. At least when the meal was on the magazine's dime.

Between bites, Donna asked her why she looked like hell and Molly ended up telling her everything. It all just spilled out. Why she couldn't be with Cam. That he was a perfect escort. But he was leaving. And there was no denying she wasn't a family kind of person. So why was she even thinking about it? Worst of all, she hadn't told Cam about returning his trading card.

By the time Molly was done, Donna had finished her omelet and her plate had been cleared. Molly's hollandaise sauce had hardened, and she was on her third coffee.

"You done wallowing?" Donna asked.

Molly sighed and nodded.

"You're an idiot."

"Thanks. That means a lot, coming from you." Molly wouldn't cry, even though she wanted to.

"If that lower lip keeps quivering, I swear to God I'm going to walk right out of here. I know you haven't slept, but you need to pay attention now."

The volume of those last few words had a sobering effect. So did finishing her Americano.

"All work and no play makes Molly a dumb ass," Donna said. "You've got a gorgeous man at your beck and call, according to your own caffeine-frenzied words, he's 'freaking unbelievable in bed,' and he's got a built-in expiration date. Where's the downside?"

Molly opened her mouth, but no words came out. She'd just finished telling her the downside. Hadn't Donna been listening?

"Yes, I know that he's leaving. And because he's leaving and you're dead set on being the next international wine guru, you're going to watch him go. But you have him for a few more months. Even though you think you have to work every single minute you're awake, you actually don't. In fact, it's not healthy."

"I've gotten this far because I haven't let up."

"I understand. But there's a thing called 'filling the well.' The only new wines you're tasting are at events where you're working or that I'm giving you. That's not okay. Take a week off. Go visit the vineyards in Vermont. If you can pull the money together, go to Washington and Oregon. Have Phillip fly you out to Bordeaux. God knows he's rich enough."

"Donna. Be real. I've got classes. The show. I'm going to the Long Island Wine Camp, so that's something."

Donna signaled the waitress and asked her to take Molly's coffee cup away and bring her a large glass of water. "Have you invited him?"

"It's for three days."

Donna gave her a look that made Molly wince. "And?"

"It would be asking too much."

"Wait. Explain that to me. It's too many days? It's too big a favor to ask? Or it feels too risky?"

Molly felt the heat spread from her cheeks. "Yes. All of that."

"Sweetheart." Donna's voice softened as she leaned in and looked at her over the top of her glasses. "You're allowed."

Okay, Molly really had had too much coffee because that didn't make any sense at all. "Huh?"

"You're allowed to have fun. To take time off for you. To take risks with your heart. To find out who you are besides what Phillip and Simone told you to be."

"That's not fair—"

"Forget that last part. That's none of my business. But I'm your friend, and I like to think I'm also a mentor."

"Of course you are. You've been wonderful. Without you I'd—"

"You'd have done great. Because you're good at whatever you put your mind to. I don't want you to regret this. Broken hearts mend. Lost opportunities never heal. Cameron's a good guy. Maybe you can give yourself permission to enjoy him while you can."

"Don't you think he should have a chance to meet someone who could be the right woman?"

"That's his business and his problem. Frankly, I don't care. I don't love *him*."

Molly's breath caught. Did that mean— Had Donna just said she loved her? She'd been a good friend and, yes, definitely a mentor, but— Molly looked down at her trembling hands. "You know how you can tell if a person's grown up in foster care?"

"How's that?"

She looked up and met Donna's gaze. "They don't know how to react when people are being wonderful."

Donna put her hand on Molly's. "It's a learned skill, and you're as smart as they come. Let people in. Invite that man to the Hamptons. And for God's sake, tell him what you did about the trading card. He'll understand. I promise."

THE CAFFEINE JITTERS had settled down, which just left her regular jitters. Calling Cam after their weird phone conversation wasn't easy. He'd left her a message earlier, but she hadn't returned the call yet.

The meeting wasn't for another forty minutes, but she was already at the radio station. She'd found an empty office and shut herself inside to make the call, but actually pressing the right numbers wasn't as simple as Donna made it sound.

The best Molly was able to do at the moment was stare

at her Android and clench her fist. When her cell phone rang, she nearly jumped out of her seat.

It was him.

She didn't *have* to answer.

Even she couldn't believe this new level of cowardice, and she'd gotten used to ducking out on a lot of things in her time.

She pressed the tiny little telephone icon. "Hi."

"Hey," he said. Make that shouted. There was so much background noise, it was as if he were standing in the middle of Grand Central station at rush hour. "Can you hear me?"

"Yes. Where are you?"

"Aboveground train. The air conditioner is rattling. I can barely hear myself think. I know you've probably got something going on this afternoon, but I need to talk to you."

"Um, when?"

"Today. Now. Can you meet me at Coleman Playground? By Monroe and Pike?"

Molly's entire body seized up. This wasn't a simple request. Though he didn't sound mad, exactly, he must have found out about the trading card. Cam never made demands on her time.

The meeting would just be getting started. She couldn't possibly skip it. They were going to discuss her show, her time slot, her advertising budget. No one could sub for her now. This was a large part of her business plan, not something she could fool with. Today she was going to pitch the new show.

In a move she'd probably regret forever, she said, "I'll be there."

15

IT WASN'T LIKE him to be this angry. Without even giving Molly a chance to explain. But he'd been caught off guard this morning by a call from a woman from the trading-card group, and the pressure had been building ever since.

Lori had said how lucky she was to find his card, which had confused him. And her, after he'd asked if there were multiple cards for the same person. She'd explained that there was only one, but the cards could be returned if things hadn't worked out.

He'd turned the date down, of course. He had no desire to meet Lori or anyone else. The problem was he'd thought Molly had felt the same way.

What the hell had happened?

He thought back to last night's stilted phone call. Obviously the mistake she'd been reluctant to talk about was him. That they shouldn't have had sex. That they shouldn't have even gone out together.

That she was willing to interrupt her precious schedule to meet him without knowing why seemed to confirm his suspicion.

He saw her, dressed in business clothes, walking across the grass toward him. Disappointment and hurt took over from anger. Behind him, his team was getting warmed up for their softball game. His sisters were here; so was his dad. Could be the best or worst time to have their talk—he had no idea. But he'd been asked to sub for one of their bartenders and talking to Molly in person couldn't wait.

"Hi," she said with a tentative smile.

He put his arm around her...only because his family would be watching. Not because it felt like the most natural thing in the world. Without hesitating she slid her arm around his waist, and he wondered if she still felt something, too. Or was she just playing her part?

"Molly!" Emmy said, her voice so cheerful, Cam felt like smacking someone.

"Hey," Molly said, giving her an anemic wave.

"Glad you made it. Cam's been moping around like he lost his pet koala." Emmy turned to her dad. "Remember that koala bear? He carried it everywhere. Couldn't live without it. What did he call it?"

"Woger," Gordon said. "Had a little trouble with his *R*s for a while." He winked at Molly, who smiled and blushed.

"I'm standing right here," Cam said.

"It's nice," Molly said, her voice subdued, her eyes avoiding contact. "I like hearing about what you were like when you were young."

Cam stared at her for a moment then turned to the team. "When are we starting this damn game? It's hot as hell out here, and I have work to do back at the brewery."

"Wow," Amber said, raising her eyebrows as she repositioned her cap. "Someone's still grouchy."

Cameron bit back a curse and led Molly toward the bleachers. There was a shady area that wasn't crowded. Mostly because hardly anyone was crazy enough to watch the game in this heat. Not as insane as they were for playing, but that was his sisters in a nutshell.

"Can I get you a drink?"

Molly smiled. "Anything that isn't alcoholic would be great. Thanks."

He looked at her for a long moment, wishing things hadn't gotten all twisted up. Before he could stop himself, he leaned in and kissed her as though he meant it. As though he'd missed her. As though he wanted her.

She kissed him back as if she wanted him, too. Not fair.

He got her a soda from the cooler, and before he could launch a conversation, he heard his name being called. "Unbelievable," he muttered. "Today they start on time."

"Go," Molly said. "I'll be here waiting."

There weren't many breaks to be had, even though it was just a bar league. Not because of any formal rules, but because of his family. Talk about hypercompetitive. He figured he'd sneak away for a few minutes when his team went up to bat.

His plan failed. It didn't help that he was a lousy right fielder and an even lousier batter. He normally didn't give a damn, but the chatter was getting on his last nerve. And there was Molly, sweating in the heat. He was still angry, but he hadn't planned on torturing her.

She kept offering him smiles. Quick looks that would skitter away when caught.

Finally, it was the seventh inning, and after that they'd take a break. He was up at bat, and he swung away at two balls that were both high and inside. The third swing, something happened. A crack followed by a jolt that went straight up his arms. It took him a few seconds to realize he needed to run. Fast as he could. Past first, straight on to second, where Carlos waved like a madman from the third-base line, screaming at him to run, goddammit, run!

That he was tagged out just before making it home was such an obvious metaphor for the way his life had been going, it wasn't even funny.

AFTER THE LONGEST game in history was finally over, Cam headed her way. He looked wonderful in his old jeans and Four Sisters T-shirt. He'd switched out the batting helmet for his baseball cap, and Molly's chest ached at the thought that she might never see him like this again.

"You were much better out there than you'd led me to believe," she said. "I thought for sure you'd make that home run."

Shrugging, he climbed up to the third row, where she was sitting, her new diet soda in hand. It was hot, she was tired and nervous, and watching him with his family had done a number on her head.

For all their yelling and posing, the game hadn't been about winning. She'd learned a couple of things from talking to the only other Four Sisters fan: that one of the guys from the brewery side was actually a much better fielder and batter than Cam, but Cam was the one they'd dragged to the park. That Gordon hadn't played at all, but he'd cheered his kids and his team as if he were watching the World Series.

They were a *family.* It wasn't just the title; it was the way they saw the world. They missed their sister who lived in Indiana. Emmy had spent half her time holding up her cell phone so Ruby could hear all the action.

After Cam's disappointing out, Emmy had hugged him, sort of. Just one arm around his shoulders and a pat on the back. Amber had given him a noogie. All the while, Molly had been in tears. Not sobbing or anything that dramatic. Just a combination of exhaustion and regret. She'd messed things up so badly.

With everything so confused, she found herself wishing for things that made no sense. That she was part of this stupid softball team, even though she couldn't play and wasn't associated with the bar. That she was the kind of woman who would want a family of her own.

"You returned my card," Cam said without preamble. He didn't seem mad or irritable as he had earlier. Maybe the physical exercise had mellowed him. Or maybe he just didn't care.

He was sitting close but not touching her. She swallowed a lump of pure emotion and said, "I got scared."

"Scared. Of me?"

"Of us." She pushed her hair back from her face when all she wanted to do was use it to hide. "I was worried that I was losing my edge. I'd been thinking about you so much, I started making mistakes."

He looked at her, not smiling, just waiting.

"At work. I made a bad call on a wine at a tasting that was important. I got confused about who I was talking to on the show. That interview I mentioned the other day? I blew it. Badly. And I freaked out. I put the card back in the pile. Two minutes later, I realized it was a mistake. Unfortunately, it was already gone."

"Uh, yeah. Someone named Lori called this morning."

She covered her face, embarrassment making her warm skin hotter. When she was ready, she sat up straighter and looked him right in the eye. "I'm sorry. I should have said something last night. I was a coward."

"Look, if it's interfering with your work, we can stop. I mean it. I like you. A lot. I'd prefer to go on like we have been. But I won't be collateral damage."

He was completely serious and had every right to be. It fit now, why he'd asked her to come here today when he was fully aware of her schedule. Their whole relationship up until now had revolved around her. He'd been so accommodating, bending to her life, her rules.

But now the rules had changed. She'd changed them by her actions. His ultimatum made perfect sense, and while her knee-jerk reaction was to immediately insist she didn't want to stop, she forced herself to think it through.

Donna's advice aside, if Molly continued with Cam there were things to consider outside of fantastic sex and having a great escort. While she wouldn't have to drop everything for him, she'd need to compromise. Not just that, she'd need to *want* to compromise, or else she'd end up resenting him. Them.

"Okay," he said, his expression flat and unfamiliar. "I'll take that as a goodbye."

"No. No, I was just—" She could barely breathe. "Are you going out with Lori?"

He seemed startled at first. "No," he said, smiling his crooked grin. "Would that have made you jealous?"

"Shut up," she muttered and leaned against him.

"Not a goodbye, then?" As she shook her head, she kissed him, hoping he would accept it as the apology it was.

His smile, when they separated, let her breathe again. "Come to the Hamptons with me next week," she whispered.

"The Long Island Wine Camp?"

"Yeah." She teased his bottom lip between her teeth and didn't let go until he moaned. "It would mean being gone for a few days."

He still hadn't moved away. They were talking into each other's mouths and she couldn't get enough of it. Kisses peppered each sentence. Even though it was perfect, it made her want so much more.

"I'm sure I can get the time off. I know the boss."

She smiled even though she'd have to work harder than ever to keep her career on track.

"BEST WINE CAMP I've ever been to."

Molly grinned as she looked up into Cameron's gaze. "It's the only wine camp you've been to."

"Doesn't matter. The wine's great. The food's great. But the best part is making out with you on the beach."

He'd been telling her wonderful things since they'd arrived Monday afternoon. Although the camp went until Friday, her participation lasted only until Wednesday, which was a damn shame. "I can't argue with that. I'd been a making-out-on-the-beach virgin before today, with no idea what I was missing." She lifted her head so she could reach his lips, and he brought his mouth back down to hers.

The heat of the late-afternoon sun would have been unbearable if not for the breeze. She hadn't been to the ocean much. Especially not as an adult. That situation would change from this day forward. At least as long as Cam was in Queens and the weather held.

He stopped midkiss when sounds other than the waves and the gulls intruded into their secluded patch of sand. They'd not only been discovered, but invaded by a crowd of teenagers who had no problem walking within an inch of where they were sitting and kicking sand on their towels.

"Hey, watch it." Cameron pulled her closer until the rowdy idiots passed them. "You okay?"

"Yeah. I think making out by the shore is now my favorite thing. Second favorite."

Cam sat up, brushing sand off his chest. He sure as hell looked good in his trunks. When she'd first seen them, she'd had to hide a laugh. They had birds all over them in a pattern she'd have associated more with a kid than a man. He'd just shrugged and said most of his things were in storage.

He continued to be adorable in offbeat ways, and she wondered if his ease with himself was something inherent in his personality or was a result of being part of a big family. Naturally, she'd always assumed her paralyzing shyness as a child had to do with being an orphan. The nature vs. nurture questions were always more complex when there had been no nurturing at all.

"What's that look?" he asked.

"Nothing. Just wondering how come some fabulous woman hasn't already married you. You're not exactly a spring chicken."

"Hey. I resent that. I'm a spring rooster, and don't you forget it."

She clucked at him just as a couple jogged close enough to their towels to overhear. Weirdly, Molly wasn't embarrassed by their laughter at all. Not while Cameron was grinning at her as if he'd won a prize. "Seriously," she said. "You're gorgeous and smart and you have an amazing sense of humor. There must've been someone."

He sobered a bit as she sat up. They hadn't brought chairs, just towels and sunscreen, so they settled cross-legged facing each other. "I had a girlfriend for a while. We met at MIT. She was working on her master's thesis in mathematics while I was finishing up my PhD."

"Why don't you call yourself Dr. Crawford?"

"They do at work, but in Queens?" He snorted. "You don't think I get enough grief from my sisters? Are you getting hungry? I think I might be getting hungry."

"Dinner's in a couple of hours, and stop changing the subject. What happened between you and the mathematician?"

"I could point out that you changed the— Never mind. We lived together for three years and then we split up. We shouldn't have stuck it out so long. I knew from the beginning that she wasn't the one, but the arrangement was comfortable for both of us."

"How did you know she wasn't the one?"

He shrugged. "The same way everyone knows. No magic. The chemistry wasn't there."

"Magic?" He couldn't have surprised her more if he'd told her their star signs weren't in alignment. "You're a scientist. How on earth do you believe in the magic of love?"

"It's because I'm a chemist." He tapped his temple. "Love happens right here. It's all chemistry. We're attracted to people who fit the blueprints of our expectations and early coding. The best matches and the greater chance of healthy offspring are predictable according to scent reactions. There are different cues, if you know how to look for them, in sexual responses versus mating responses, especially in males." He smiled at her stunned expression. "Okay, I admit it. I use the term *magic* as shorthand, but it's still about the right chemicals firing in the right way when you meet the perfect person to be with forever."

Molly was surprised her jaw didn't drop to her lap. "That is the most bizarre combination of fact and romanticized nonsense I've ever heard in my life. There's not just one person you meet and, boom, you've got a life partner forever. Who told you that, and how could you be a doctor and not see how ridiculous that is?"

He clearly didn't appreciate her opinion, and she supposed she could have been more tactful, but seriously? "Okay, tell me this. What, exactly, made you decide you wanted to stick with me, even though you knew I was leaving?"

"Lots of things. Your personality. You make me laugh, and not just at you."

"Very amusing." He gestured for her to go on.

"You're sexy, and you have strengths where I have weaknesses."

"And I smell great, right?"

She burst out laughing. "You smell great?"

"I'm not kidding around. Everything you just said was a result of chemical interactions plus early conditioning. The only exception might be that I just happen to find it easy to talk to strangers, but I'm pretty sure there's a neurological basis for that, as well."

She stared at him. "Are you saying I'm…?" She couldn't quite finish, certain she'd misunderstood.

He looked away. "You've come the closest."

"I'm not sure how to take that."

He met her gaze again, and while she could read the discomfort in his expression, he didn't back down. "It's not personal. It's not. Again, it's biology. Which is actually our saving grace. Because if we were a perfect match, we'd have to make some huge compromises. Can you see yourself living in Syracuse and still having the career you want?"

Molly swallowed so hard, she nearly choked. The day she'd returned his card she'd wondered that very thing. God, she should never have questioned his cockeyed belief. "Who says I'd be the one to have to compromise?" She purposely made it sound as if she was teasing.

"You're right. It could also mean that I'd have to give up my work with Protean Pharmaceuticals, and that would be like cutting off an arm. My whole life I've wanted to make a difference in this world, so either way we'd be screwed."

"For the record, I'm not sure whether I should be insulted," she said, hoping to lighten things up, especially after hearing what his work meant to him.

"You know exactly what I'm talking about. That's why you didn't want to have sex before you found out I was leaving. You knew, instinctively, that we were at risk."

Her stomach somersaulted. What was that saying about the truth hurting? "You make it sound like love is a virus."

"Maybe it is. Just not the kind we tend to think about."

She pushed herself forward until she was balanced on her knees and they were inches away from a kiss. "You need to work on your dirty talk. Now, how about we go back to the room and take a shower together? See what kind of chemical fusion we can ignite."

"That makes no sense, but points for trying."

"I'm going to fall over in a moment if you don't kiss me."

He obliged.

But she fell anyway.

DESPITE MAKING LOVE before and after dinner, Cameron was wide-awake. The conversation on the beach kept poking at him. As did the trading-card mix-up. Molly lay beside him, so beautiful and peaceful in sleep.

He couldn't get enough of her, and that was a problem. The fake-girlfriend thing had stopped being fake a while ago, but he hadn't realized that his feelings for her meant there was a fundamental flaw in his thinking.

She'd shaken something loose in his beliefs. He'd held on to his idea of chemical attraction and finding *the one* like a dying man held on to a lifeline. For the past hour, he'd traced the notion back. It had formed before he'd moved to Syracuse. Before MIT. Hell, before high school.

Then it had hit him. The magic-of-love theory had been a bedtime story. Literally. How could he have forgotten that? He'd heard it from his father over and over. Cam remembered his dad crying, tears running down his cheeks even as he smiled.

Then he'd heard the same story from Ruby when she was in charge of helping him go to sleep.

The narrative had become part of his worldview, unexamined as a fact.

Cam reeled at his own stupidity. The irony that he had a PhD in chemistry seemed particularly cruel. Almost as brutal as the real truth of his situation with Molly.

16

DOING IT WITH the lights on had become a thing since their first night together in Long Island. Now that they were back in his apartment, they continued the practice. The best part was when their eyes met. She supposed that was why they always seemed to end up in the missionary position. She wished there was another name for it. Something that sounded more intimate.

"Christ, the way you look at me," he said, moving inside her with steady, slow pressure. Her legs were wrapped around his hips, her hands sliding across his tanned back, their breath mingling with contented sighs.

"Tell me," she said, lifting her chin as he shifted just enough for him to push in deeper.

"You look as if you don't want to be anywhere else."

"Of course I don't."

Cam shook his head, a quick correction. "No. I meant like you don't want to be *anywhere* else. Or with anyone else." He stroked her cheek with the pad of his thumb. "Do me a favor? Don't close your eyes."

She smiled, understanding what he wanted, although she wasn't sure she could deliver. "I'll do my best."

He pulled out again, almost all the way, but this time when he reentered her, he went in hard.

Her gasp was loud enough that it carried over the noise from the pub's jukebox below them. His attention, his desire and, frankly, his stamina had been astonishing. After the long drive home this afternoon she'd have thought he'd want to get some rest, but no. He'd wanted her, and she'd wanted him right back.

Tomorrow they'd return to the real world and she'd be busier than ever. So tonight they would connect in every way possible. Tightening her grip around him as the stirrings began low and deep inside her, all her muscles tensed in preparation. He clearly felt her because he drove into her so hard, the bed bounced against the wall. Her world narrowed to the space they shared, his eyes bright with fire even as she struggled to keep hers from closing.

When she came, she nearly jerked out of his grasp, but he held her tight, saying her name over and over. But a moment later, when he came, it didn't matter that her eyes were open, because his were squeezed shut.

He took his first real breath and the lights went out. So did the vibrations from downstairs. His fridge and AC stopped humming until all that could be heard were their panting breaths. The power was out.

"It'll probably come back on in a minute," Cam said.

She didn't care about the lights, but the air-conditioning was another matter. Even with it blasting in his apartment, they were both sweating, especially where they'd rubbed together.

He flopped on his back. Now that she had a few of her wits about her, she realized how profound the darkness was. The moon was a sliver and wouldn't have been able to fight through the clouds.

"Wonder if it's just the block?" she asked.

"If it lasts ten minutes, I'll go down. Help with crowd control."

"I thought you had a generator?"

"For the brewery, not the bar. We've got a lot of flashlights and candles, though. It'll be fun for a while yet, but then, who knows. Things could get tricky."

She nodded, knowing he couldn't see. "We should probably go help. Or at least put some clothes on."

"What? Clothes?" Cam pulled her in close, kissed her but missed the mark, landing more on the side of her nose than her lips. "I never said anything about clothes."

"Hush, you. I assume you have supplies up here?"

"Oh, all right," he said. "If we must. I'll get the flashlights. You sit tight."

INSIDE, THE BAR was already a swamp. They kept the place cool, sure, but a lot of that came from all the overhead circular fans, which weren't working. Cam made sure Molly was right in front of him as they let the flashlight guide them to the service bar. Everything felt and looked weird in the dark. The emergency lights were on, showing the exits, the bathrooms, the service area. Most tables had already been provided with lanterns, although Cam knew they didn't have enough for all of them.

Molly sidled up next to him, her arm around his waist. "Are people going to walk out on their bills?"

"Yep."

"That's not very nice."

"Nope, it's not. It won't kill us, and it's not going to be that many. The locals won't. Especially because we do keep the taps running. The real mess is going to be in the kitchen. We have to put as much of the food in the big fridge as we can, as quickly as possible. If this blackout goes on for a long time, we could lose it all."

"Ouch," she said. "That's got to hurt."

"There's insurance, but that's mostly to protect the brewery. First, though, I'm going to see if they need me in the kitchen. Then I'll come back and help out here."

They'd reached the bar, where he spotted his dad, Amber and—oh, yeah, Ruby. His oldest sister was here for a conference, and she hadn't met Molly yet. The whole crew wore glow-in-the-dark necklaces, which helped a great deal.

"Molly," Amber said, her smile appearing truly evil with the green glow coming up from around her neck. "Didn't know you were here, but we could sure use the help if you're up for it."

"Okay," she said and looked at Cam.

He kissed her. "You don't have to. You can just stick with me until this thing's over."

"No, it's all right," she said, her voice lowered like his. "But thanks."

Cam was hesitant to leave. This situation was the kind of thing Molly hated, and he was abandoning her. He'd just have to take care of things quickly. For all he knew, the kitchen staff might not even need him. "I'll be back soon."

"Don't worry, bro," Amber said. "We'll be fine."

The last he saw of Molly, she was putting a yellow necklace on while Amber held out a flashlight. Molly nodded as Amber talked, and it was all he could do not to push people out of the way so he could reach the kitchen.

He needn't have worried. Karla, the pub's head cook, was handling things like the pro she was. Most of the food was already in the fridge, and the extra thermometers were in plain sight. The ovens and stove were shut down. Everything looked to be in order.

He should go and see about the brewery, though.

"Don't worry about it," Karla said just as he reached the

door. "Eric's got everything locked up tight. He called the power company, and it's going to be a long night. A big section of Queens is down. They don't expect the power to be up again until tomorrow morning."

"Well, damn. That's not good."

He could see her silhouette but not her expression, although he doubted she would look anything but serene. Karla was in her forties, had four kids, and her husband had left her with enough gambling debts to make anyone insane. She'd turned to yoga, meditation and cooking. "It'll all be fine as long as no one tries to get behind the wheel drunk," Karla said.

"I'm on it. Thanks."

He grabbed himself a glow necklace on his way back to the taproom—yellow, like Molly's. She wasn't standing behind the bar. It took him a few minutes to find her out among the tables. She had a pitcher in one hand and a flashlight in the other.

A bump to his shoulder made him turn. "I was hoping to meet your girl, and now it's too busy for me to even have a quick chat. Is she staying for the night?"

It was Ruby. "Hey, Cam," he said, his voice high and mocking. "Long time no see. How are you?"

"Yeah, yeah, you're a sight for sore eyes. Now tell me about the love of your life. I want details."

"She's not the love of my life," he said.

"That's not what I've been hearing."

"You believe what you hear in this family, you deserve the consequences. I like her. A lot. But the most important thing in her life is her career. And since the same goes for me, things are just perfect between us."

Dammit. The moment the words were spoken, he wanted to call them back. He needed Ruby to believe that he and Molly had a future.

"Well, that's a crock of bull," Ruby said. "You're not that complex, Cam. Sorry. Wish you were, but we all know you want to get married, have kids. The puzzle is how you've held out for so long."

"How are the taps doing?" he asked, not willing to go there.

"You're no fun anymore. Fine. The lager is getting gassy. I'd shut her down if I were you. Maybe get some of these freeloaders to go home."

"I'm gonna go check on Molly, so if you could take care of the lager, I'd appreciate it."

Cameron headed through the crowd, and it wasn't an easy trip. Plenty of locals meant he was stopped at virtually every table. Not many people had heard the news about how big the outage was, so he left a trail of bitching and moaning behind him. Unfortunately, a lot of folks were going to stay until there was no more draft available, and that was when he and his dad would have to stand guard at the doors, making sure that no one did anything stupid.

Finally, he reached Molly. He stood back, watching and listening as she finished pouring the last of her pitcher into a glass, all the while telling the patrons about the difference between the fructose sugars in wine versus the maltose sugars in beer and how they both fed the yeast that turned into alcohol.

Her voice was animated and the people at the table were either interested or too stunned to stop her. When she finished her explanation, instead of asking if she could get anyone anything else, she asked, "Any questions?"

He wanted to kiss her. Right now. In front of everyone.

As if she could hear his grin, she turned. "You're here already. I thought you'd be in the kitchen longer."

"I'm just the guy with the recipes. Everyone else does the real work around here."

"So did you guys go to school together or something?" someone asked.

Cam aimed his flashlight around the table and found Manuel and Rita, bikers who'd made The Four Sisters a home away from home. "Nope. She's a wine expert. A master sommelier, in fact. If you were smart, you'd stop drinking beer and ask her to pick you out a nice red. You won't get better advice."

Rita looked up at Molly. "You got something good that's not expensive?"

"I don't know. I haven't seen the cellar."

"I'll show you." He took the pitcher from her and asked the table, "Anyone else want a glass?"

Two other women at the table said they did. Cam was sure that said something telling about his gender, but he wasn't going to try to figure out what tonight. "We'll be back. Also, the power's most likely not going to come on till morning, so don't plan on riding out if you can't pass the Breathalyzer."

This time, the bitching and moaning were about him, not the power outage.

MOLLY ENDED UP serving more wine than she had since she'd worked at Barndiva as an assistant sommelier. The selection of reds was good for a brewpub, but she had some ideas as to how they could make it great without it costing them an arm and a leg.

As she made the rounds, checking on the patrons, she talked mostly about wine, which was easy for her. But she also talked about other things. Not just the lights being out, either. Maybe small talk was easier in the dark.

She'd made a whole table laugh, and the joke had been spontaneous, about Cam. She hadn't been mean. She wouldn't. But everyone at the table had known him for years, and they were telling her things, and her joke just…fit.

It wouldn't have occurred to her that people would stay and drink during a power outage. It was hotter inside than outside, which she discovered only when Cam pulled her out the door.

"There's a breeze," she said.

He wasn't holding her, but she knew he wanted to. "Do you know what time it is?"

"No."

"Late. You should have been asleep hours ago. I haven't looked at your schedule, but I think you're booked from seven-thirty in the morning on tomorrow. Right?"

"Yes, you're right," she said. "But it's okay. Nobody expects a huge blackout."

"Let me take you upstairs, put you to bed."

She lifted the hair off her neck and cursed her foolishness for not putting it up ages ago. "You're not staying with me?"

"I want to, but there are too many drunken people for me to leave."

"Then I'll stay, too. And we'll make sure everyone gets home safely."

He touched her. His hand on her arm. Sliding up to her shoulder, the back of her neck. "It's almost one. We probably won't close for at least another hour. There'll be taxis to call. Someone'll probably need to drive folks home in the van, and I won't let my dad do it, so…"

"I'll stay," she said. "I've done all-nighters before. I didn't die."

"Yeah, but anything you don't finish tomorrow you'll add to the pile you've already got for the next day. You can't work like that. I'm worried you'll fall over in the middle of a meeting and I won't be there to catch you."

She pulled his hand down and held it. "Thank you, but I don't think I can sleep right now. I'm too wired. You realize you're going to have to restock your wine stores. And did I tell you I had them pay for every glass? I had to make change, but Ruby helped. I think Amber's pissed because Ruby was supposed to be helping her. Also, um, I'm pretty sure Ruby's drunk."

He laughed. "I heard you were telling jokes about me. Do I want to know what you said?"

"Probably not."

"Okay. Nothing's sacred around here anyway. Thanks about the money. I hope they all tipped you well."

"I kept those in a separate pocket, so we can give them to the staff. I only saw a few of them leave. Are they always this loyal?"

"They're family. We stick together—in baseball, in blackouts. Anything beginning with a *B*."

She raised his hand to her lips. "We'll see the night through, and I'll cancel my first meeting. It's with Rox-anne, and everything's going to be wonky tomorrow anyway. She won't mind. I'll ask her to lunch. Voilà. A solution."

He touched her face, lightly drawing a map across her features, and then he kissed her. Perfectly centered on her lips, his tongue slipped inside her mouth and they stood there for a long while, rocking in the faint breeze with ac-tual, visible stars in the sky above them. God, she liked touching him. She didn't even care that by gripping his fine ass with both hands, she was giving him a burgeon-ing erection.

"What if the lights come on all of a sudden?" he said. "Everyone will know what we've been doing out here."

"It's their own fault for staying so late. Don't these people have jobs?"

"Ah, now we're talking Queens logic. The whole neigh-borhood will milk this blackout to death. Half of them won't go to work today, and the other half won't get any work done because they'll spend the whole day talking about the blackout. Except *we'll* have to work, because most of them will come in for a cold beer to hash it out again. That or they'll stay home making babies, and there'll be a huge uptick in births nine months from now."

"I see. It's very complicated to live here, isn't it?"

"Not so much. Mostly, we're a bunch of regular joes, and then there are the outliers. Great people who came from humble beginnings."

"Like you, you mean?" She kissed him again, didn't want him to stop talking, though.

"No, I mean like Simon and Garfunkel. Johnny Ramone. Lucy Liu."

"You'll be on that list someday, and I'll name-drop you every chance I get."

"The hell with the bar," he said, his voice lower and closer. "Let's go back upstairs."

She wanted to. But going back inside had its appeal, too. She still had her neon yellow necklace on, and that made her staff. That made her family. At least until the lights came on.

17

MOLLY HADN'T SEEN Cameron since the blackout. Today that would be fixed, because he was not only coming to the station to watch her radio show, but they would both be going back to her apartment for a couple of hours afterward.

As predicted, staying at The Four Sisters through the outage had done a number on her, but she'd worked feverishly to catch up on her work since then, and finally, *finally* she'd be getting her reward.

Cam had let her know he was going to arrive about fifteen minutes after the start of the show. He was so excited about being in the studio, she'd had to warn him that he'd probably get bored five minutes in.

It didn't mean a thing that she'd gotten dressed up, either. She always tried to look professional and nice, but this morning she'd been especially careful with her makeup, had worn her slinky green dress that made the red in her hair stand out and was even wearing the small diamond earrings Phillip and Simone had given her when she'd achieved her master-sommelier certification.

She got herself settled in her booth and waited for things to get started, but clearly time had decided to slow to a crawl just to spite her. So she occupied herself with wondering if

Cam would be free to accompany her to the Food & Wine Festival in October. The magazine was hosting a suite at the Marriott, and Donna had said she'd be willing to let Molly stay there, even though it was Donna's year to claim the right.

A fancy suite in a big hotel with plenty of fantastic wine to see them through the night? It sounded like heaven.

When she got her first call, she was still grinning. "Hi, Trisha. What kind of food are you looking to pair with wine?"

"Wow, you sound happy, Molly."

"I do?"

"Yeah. Have you been doing some wine tasting out there at WNYU?"

"No, but great idea. I should keep a few bottles on hand. Sip away during the program. Imagine how interesting the pairing ideas would get by the end of the show."

Trisha laughed and Molly joined in, which wasn't her style. In fact, Roxanne and Bobby were both staring at her as if she were drunk. Molly didn't give them a second glance.

"I'm having people over for fondue," Trisha said. "I got this ancient set from my parents. I think they used it in the '70s for parties, so I'm hosting a theme night. I should probably serve white wine, but I don't know what kind to choose. For dessert I'm doing chocolate with fruit and marshmallows. The cheese fondue has Swiss and Gruyère cheeses, as well as white wine in it, so I'm not sure if I'm supposed to serve the same wine I cook with. And the recipe also calls for kirsch, and I don't know what kirsch is."

"Is that the only savory fondue you're making?"

"No, I'm also doing a hot-oil one with beef and fried potatoes."

In the reflection of the window between her studio and

the booth, Molly saw the door open behind her. Cam came in and closed it very quietly, then moved over to the couch. She couldn't acknowledge him now, but she wasn't able to stop her smile. "Sounds fabulous. Okay, first, kirsch is a clear fruit brandy traditionally made from double distillation of dark sour cherries. As for the wine in the cheese fondue, I'd go with a nice American Sauvignon Blanc. To serve with that, you might want something fruitier. Off dry, like a Riesling or a Chenin Blanc."

Molly made it through the rest of the conversation without screwing up, which was amazing, considering she never looked away from Cam's reflection.

When they finally went to commercial, he waited until she gave him a nod, then he spun her chair around and gave her a kiss that would fuel Bobby's fantasies for a long time.

Not that she wanted to think about Bobby's fantasies. The rest of the program seemed to fly by, and even though she wanted to hear Cam's reaction to the show, they barely spoke the whole distance to the subway. They were both too busy just being happy.

DRESSED ONLY IN his boxers, Cam was still too hot to put on the rest of his clothes. He wasn't even sure he wanted to go out for dinner, but Molly had a craving for Thai curry, and there wasn't a good place near her apartment that delivered. Hard to believe in this day and age, but if Molly wanted curry, she'd have it.

While he waited for her to finish in the bathroom, he wandered over to take a glance at her whiteboard. His mood plummeted when he saw how little room for him there was on it. Needing a distraction, he popped open one of the cupboard doors above her bed. He half expected the door to be a facade, but it wasn't. There was a real space

behind it crammed to the hilt, mostly with toilet paper, but
there were about five boxes of soap, a handful of tooth-
brushes in their packaging and a stack of toothpaste boxes.

The next cupboard was equally stuffed with feminine
supplies, shampoo, deodorant and cotton balls. Small as her
place was, it seemed to him she'd gone overboard stock-
ing multiples of everything. Even six bags of SweeTarts.

He closed the cupboard doors and sat down on her bed
as the revelation sank in. He'd seen this before. A friend
of Emmy's had been a foster kid and a hoarder. She used
to sock away everything she could because at the group
homes, the smaller kids were often left without because
the older kids stole everything they could.

He kept forgetting Molly had grown up without a family. Even given the absence of his mother, there'd never
been a day in his life when he'd gone without. He hadn't
always gotten what he'd wanted, but he'd always had everything he needed.

When his gaze traveled back over to her impossible
schedule, written across the whiteboard that was the most
important piece of furniture in the room, it made a new
kind of sense. She wasn't just ambitious for the sake of
getting writing awards and good press. She was building
a foundation for the rest of her life.

Here he was, with choices everywhere he looked. A se-
cure future with a major pharmaceutical firm. A guaran-
teed job working for the family business. He had access
to excellent medical care, a retirement plan, a savings account.

How much could Molly be making at each of her jobs?
Enough to stock up on essentials, but not quite enough for
healthy meals? Definitely not enough that she could afford
to stand still for more than a few minutes.

It was a hell of a wake-up call. He absolutely couldn't

ask her to change her plans so often. From this moment onward, she would call the shots, and when she had time for him, he'd be damn glad of it.

The urge to rescue her was strong, though. To make sure she had enough money every week, to never let her go through another day being scared that she wouldn't have enough.

But she wouldn't want that. Not charity. He just had to take one look at her work ethic. A person like her would be insulted at the very thought.

But screw it—they weren't going dutch anymore. No matter how much she insisted.

The door opened, and his heart swelled seeing her walk out in her underwear. Nothing fancy. Of course they wouldn't be fancy.

HER OFFICE AT *Wine Connoisseur* wasn't really *her* office so much as a spare office, but it didn't matter. They had few full-time employees, and most of them concerned themselves with the online side of things. Molly figured they'd soon stop publishing the print copies altogether, except perhaps an annual issue.

She finished off her column about the Fairview South African Cyril Black Shiraz, and halfway through her second read, her mind switched to Cameron and the last time she'd seen him. It was only three days ago, but it had been a quickie lunch break at her place. Three days was too long. Even though they spoke on the phone every chance they had, it wasn't enough.

Catching up with work had been harder than she'd expected, mostly because she was having trouble focusing. It wasn't just the lack of sleep that sent her mind wandering. It was Cam.

She missed him. A phone call would be wonderful, but

she wanted to write at least one more column in the next hour, then grab some lunch on the way to her afternoon classes at NYU. It continued to get more difficult to shrink him, though. She'd long ago given up the idea of stuffing him away in her thought box, not since he'd become larger than life to her. That was a weird and troubling thought she had no time to analyze.

The knock on the office door stole her attention. "Come in," she said, expecting to see Donna.

Instead, Phillip and Simone walked in, and Molly thought she must have fallen asleep. She had to be dreaming because they couldn't be here. Not on a Friday morning in the East Village.

"Surprise," Simone said.

Oh, God. Molly rushed to give them kisses on both cheeks. "What are you doing here?"

"We've got some appointments in New York, and next Sunday we're off to California," Phillip said. "I'm going to tour some new vineyards on the North Coast. But we were hoping you could have lunch with us now. We've got things to talk about."

Lunch. Now. It would mean sending her copy to Donna quickly and skipping another column, which would seriously put a dent in her night, but there was no way she could say no. "Of course. Let me send this column off and we can leave. Did you have anywhere in mind?"

"We have reservations at La Birreria in twenty minutes," Simone said, and it was so wonderful to hear her voice.

"I'll hurry."

After quickly tying things up in the office, she found herself in a taxi, hating that she was in the front seat and unable to hear what was going on in the back, but soon enough they were inside the huge gourmet marketplace that was Eataly. Another short, subdued trip in the elevator to the beer garden on the roof, and they found their table was ready. Of course, they'd made the reservation for three, assuming, rightly, that Molly would drop everything as soon as they invited her.

"Where are you staying?" she asked, as Phillip looked over the wine list. She already knew that she'd have the soup and share the antipasto.

"Mondrian Soho. But that's not important. Phillip," Simone said, "tell her."

"Un moment," he said, his French pronunciation almost as good as Simone's, then turned his attention to the waitress.

Molly didn't even hear his order, she was so curious about what it was they had to say. She couldn't imagine what it could be. They wouldn't be moving back to New York; the business was too successful in France. Perhaps they were going to give her a belated gift?

Finally, they were alone again, and from the smiles the two of them kept giving each other, Molly's heart raced with anticipation.

"We've been very impressed with your last few columns," Phillip said.

She blushed. Phillip never bothered with flattery. Neither of them did. If something was good, they said so, and if it wasn't, they let her know that, too. "Thank you."

"It was no surprise to us that you won the wine-writing award. We've also heard good things about you from some of our associates. Your radio show is very popular, and you're becoming a sought-after speaker and judge."

Molly's chest tightened and it was all she could do not to let the heat behind her eyes turn into tears. This was so much better than them sending a car for the banquet.

Phillip nodded at Simone, who continued. "We'd like you to come to Bordeaux. You'll work at the vineyard to become familiar with our grapes, but mostly we'd like you to work closely with Phillip. We think you're ready to learn about the real home of wine, which you'll need to do if you're ever going to become an important voice in the industry."

Move to France? To work with Phillip?

Molly didn't say anything. She couldn't. All sorts of things were swirling inside her head. Simone, who was usually very reserved, actually seemed excited at the prospect of her moving to Bordeaux. For the first time ever, she would actually have one job that would provide her with a decent salary instead of struggling to piece together a living. Or so she assumed... "Would this be a salaried position?"

Phillip smiled. "Yes, of course."

Before Molly could ask about the compensation, Simone asked, "What do you think?"

"I'm overwhelmed." It was the truth. She hardly knew what to make of the offer.

Then there was Cam, of course. Her breath caught at the thought of him.

Simone cleared her throat, and Molly remembered she'd been asked an important question. "Thank you so much. I'm thrilled and honored. Was there a particular date you had in mind?"

"The end of October would be best. Of course, you'll need to make sure your exit is well played. Every contact is a potential ally."

The wine arrived, an excellent Soave, and Phillip raised his glass for a toast. "To the next phase of your career."

She lifted her own glass in return, but she was still reeling that they wanted her to leave so soon.

She wouldn't have three more months to get used to saying goodbye to Cameron, but six more weeks.

MOLLY'S DARK ALE for Wine Lovers was coming along
nicely. The secondary fermentation had just gotten started,
and since it was a small batch, it would be ready for presen-
tation in two weeks. The timing was perfect: in two weeks
he was escorting her to a party. After, he could bring her
back to the pub and, even though the beer would be stored
in a beer tank, he was going to surprise her with her very
own bottles. He'd even done a short run of labels so she
could keep a few. He wanted the beer to be a staple in The
Four Sisters' repertoire, to win prizes and accolades. He
wanted it to be as special as Molly herself.

Molly. They hadn't spoken since yesterday morning.
He still held out hope that she'd be able to go with him
to the Albany Charity Beer Fest tomorrow, but it didn't
seem likely. The urge was strong to whine about her lack
of availability, especially when this particular festival was
one of the most important ones for the brewery, but he was
sticking to the vow he'd made to give her all the room she
needed.

This afternoon, he'd received an email from Dr. Inaba.
Things were in motion. That was all she'd said, but that
was all he'd needed to hear. It meant that he could get a
call anytime. While he still figured, with how slowly the
wheels of the government turned, that three months was
the most likely window, in theory they could get word five
days from now. The project hadn't been tabled or thrown
out, which was good news. Hell, any motion on the part
of those committees was good news.

Sort of.

He looked around the brewery, at his friends, his coworkers. His dad was in a huddle with Eric, both men
with their baseball caps on, their arms crossed over their
chests. They weren't looking at each other, but at an empty
space by the aging tanks. That told Cam they were still

discussing the possibility of buying some bourbon barrels. They were easy to come by, what with bourbon having to be aged for two years in oak and the fact that the barrels were used only once. And because they could add a distinctive new flavor range to the beer that wasn't available from their current stock of tanks, it might be a great, cost-effective way to expand their customer base.

Cam wanted them to try a few barrels. But mostly he wanted to be here to experiment with them. Sure, he could write up potential recipes and have Eric and the others try them out, but tasting was everything. All the senses needed to be in play when using new techniques, and he was jealous that someone else would be at the controls.

He thought about staying around. Putting off going to Syracuse for a while. He was reasonably sure he could steal a few months without them having to replace him, although that might have been his ego talking.

He didn't think Dr. Inaba would mind, especially because he'd never really stopped working since he'd arrived back in Queens. He'd sent her a number of ideas and theories, and she'd been enthusiastic about several of them.

Besides, an extra few months here would give him more time with Molly. What he wasn't sure about was if she would have more time to give him.

Eric waved him over, but first Cam checked to make sure he hadn't missed a call while he'd been working. Nothing. It wasn't easy for him to wait patiently for her to call. But he wouldn't place his own call until after she finished with her NYU class.

MOLLY HAD BEEN home for half an hour, and she still hadn't called Cam. She'd been dying to tell him about being invited to go to France, but it wasn't going to be great news to him. She'd be leaving before him.

Although things between them had been a little odd lately. She'd been the one to initiate almost every call. Certainly every visit. Maybe he was just being careful not to bother her, but it felt as if Cam might be pulling back a bit.

They'd had those mad few days of the beach and the blackout when they'd been in each other's pockets, and then things had slowed to a crawl. Her fault, of course. She'd imagined they'd find a rhythm, some kind of equilibrium. They hadn't.

Calling him with news this major didn't feel right. She wanted to see him in person. Discuss it with him. But he'd be at his beer festival tomorrow. She could make a trip out there now, spend the night. But she wasn't ready.

She'd never thought she'd be the one to leave first. To cross an ocean. She'd figured Syracuse was a long way away from Brooklyn, but she could get there by train. Even work on the way up and back. It was doable. The fact that Cam would be in the same state had made all the difference. His departure wouldn't be a real goodbye.

France, on the other hand…

She dialed his number and Cam picked up on the first ring.

"If you're still awake, I assume you can't make it tomorrow."

"I'm so sorry I didn't let you know earlier. Phillip and Simone stopped by to see me on their way to California. My day has been chaos, and I can't possibly go with you tomorrow."

"Wow, that must have been quite a surprise. Hey, I'm glad you got to see them. Don't sweat it about the festival. Besides, I'll be crazy busy myself. I'd rather see you when we can actually talk and have some time to ourselves."

"Good, because I do want to see you. As soon as possible."

"I'll call you when I get home if it's not too late," he said. "Maybe we can figure something out for Sunday."

"I'd like that. And good luck tomorrow. I hope you win."

"Thanks. You get some decent sleep, huh?"

She said goodbye, then stared at her phone. She hadn't lied. But she hadn't told the whole truth, either.

As she readied herself for bed, it bothered her that she wasn't over the moon with joy and anticipation. Her thoughts were still on Cam, so of course she wasn't 100 percent thrilled. Not yet.

It wasn't a surprise, though. She'd had her chance to exit earlier and hadn't taken it, knowing this would be the result. No matter who left first, it was going to hurt. But it shouldn't break her heart.

After all, they were never meant to last.

Right?

18

THE BEER FESTIVAL was jam-packed, especially because it was held in the Albany Convention Center, where it was cool and easy to roam from booth to booth. Several members of the Four Sisters crew had driven up the day before to set up their booth and put their bottled beer on ice, but Gordon, Cam, Emmy and Amber were part of the second team that had left this morning. It had taken them more than three hours to get to the state capital and then they'd had to set up the coolers for the kegs, set out the tasting glasses and arrange the washing station. Since it wasn't their first rodeo, they managed everything in time for the grand opening, which, thank God, wasn't until eleven.

Cam had entered five beers in the competition, a couple of old favorites and three of their new seasonal brews. He expected great things from the fruit wheat and the light lager, but it was a much bigger field of competition than his last time competing here.

There was so much foot traffic that he had Tommy, the assistant manager at the brewery, rent another van and drive up all the kegs they had left of the competition beers.

Three-thirty came and went without a break for Cam,

and when his phone rang he considered letting it go to voice mail but decided to check in case it was Molly. It wasn't. He answered anyway.

"Dr. Inaba. How are you?"

"Excited. Where the hell are you, in the middle of Times Square?"

"Beer festival." He cupped the phone closer to his face. "What's going on?"

"We're a go. We not only got the funding we asked for, but we're getting the upgrades to the equipment and facility. We should be able to officially start work by the end of October, but I'd like to get a running start. It would help if you, Lasky and Schroeder could come a bit earlier."

He let that sink in for a minute. Fully funded? Upgrades? Thank God the committee had taken the forecasts seriously. But the end of next month? While he knew it was possible, he honestly hadn't expected things to move this fast. He'd have to go early anyway to find a place, get his things out of storage, buy a car. "This is great news," he said. "Outstanding."

"You'll be able to make the date?"

"Honestly, you've caught me by surprise. It's so much earlier than expected. I've got some things to wrap up here."

"I understand. Of course. You should know, though, that Dr. Becker won't be rejoining us."

Becker wasn't his favorite person, but he was their leading geneticist and his work on mutating resistant microorganisms had been critical to their research.

"But don't worry. I've known for a while, and I've been in touch with Hartig from Cambridge and Whitman from Johns Hopkins."

"Still, that's a blow to the team. Let me know who you choose and I'll study up on their work. Damn, this happened startlingly fast. I know you've worked your ass off for this. Thank you. I wish I could be more confident of my ETA, but I'll do my best to make it work."

"I'm just glad you're still part of the team. We need you there."

"Why, so you won't run out of beer?"

She laughed. "Is there a more important reason?"

"None that I can think of. I'll be in touch."

"Good. Talk to you soon. Go win some gold."

Cam put his phone away, his excitement tempered by the atmosphere. He'd been wishing all day that Molly could have been here, but now he wasn't so sure. Having a firm start date made his departure utterly real and awfully imminent. It wouldn't be the end of the world to tell his boss he was going to be delayed. She'd be fine with it. But could he really put off his arrival, knowing how much was riding on their work? Especially if the players had changed? It always took a while to get back into a working rhythm after a hiatus, and this would be even tougher.

He should be ecstatic. This was huge news, better than he'd dared hope for. But it would be difficult to leave The Four Sisters. His family.

Molly.

Of course, he'd known he'd be leaving, but the news had hit him like a blow. Which made no sense. This work was the most important thing in his life. Wasn't it?

"You gonna stand there all day, princess?" Emmy asked. "There's a line of people waiting to talk to you."

"Shut up. And that's Dr. Princess to you."

She laughed and went to refill the ice in the casks.

He didn't take another break till seven, when the judging was finished. They still had to keep serving their two-ounce samples, but Cam was ready to bolt up to the front of the auditorium if their name was called. The awards ceremony was a long one, given they had eighty-four beer categories, not to mention the prizes that went to the different types of breweries. They could have entered two more categories—best brewery and brewmaster of the year for a small brewpub—but as a group they'd decided to hang their hopes on the beer itself.

Fifteen minutes in, they won the damn gold medal for best fruit wheat beer for their Sweet Sisters Blueberry Wheat Ale. Cam was lifted off the ground by his old man, hugged to gasping by his insane sisters and given a hard smack on the back by Eric, who'd worked harder than anyone to keep the brewery running like a well-oiled machine.

Of course, he dragged his dad up to the front of the auditorium to claim the medal, but there were no speeches, not with so many awards to be handed out. But it set the tone for the rest of the night and made Cam's decisions about his future harder than ever.

THE NEXT DAY Molly arrived at The Four Sisters at a quarter to five. The atmosphere in the bar was as celebratory as expected, and all she wanted was to join in the festivities and be thrilled for Cam and the family. They'd worked so hard and accomplished so much. She was bursting with pride for Cameron, especially. It was his genius that had earned them two gold medals and two silvers.

She didn't see him. In fact, she recognized only a couple of people behind the bar, so she made her way next door to the brewery—where she found herself swept into a hug by Gordon Crawford. "Did he tell you?"

She was still dangling in his arms, her feet not touching the floor, but she managed a "Yes. Congratulations!"

before he put her down again. His smile could have lit up the city.

"He's a born brewmaster," he said. "Right from the beginning, he was all about the chemistry. He studied water properties, yeasts, carbonation, cooling, fermentation. All of it when he was just a kid in school. Probably would have gotten me in big trouble if his teacher ever found out about us making beer together. Tell you the truth, there was a time I thought I'd been a fool to let a ten-year-old try beer, but he turned out a champion. I couldn't be prouder."

Molly was grinning pretty brightly herself. Not just for Cam, but for his father, as well. He was clearly so proud of his son.

"He's upstairs, changing. It's been a mess in here, cleaning out the kegs and the cooling systems. But nobody begrudges him leaving early. Especially to be with you."

"That's a very nice thing to say."

"My son's taken his own sweet time to find the right woman, and I believe it was worth the wait. I've never seen him so happy."

Molly didn't know what to say. She'd never thought of herself as special, outside of certain wine circles. She hated that Gordon's opinion was based on a sham. Even more, that he was mistaken. Cameron hadn't found the right woman. The right woman wouldn't have chosen France over his son. Over the chance to build a family.

"Hey, you're here!"

She spun around at the sound of Cam's voice, resolving to be nothing but happy for the rest of the night. She'd tell him about her news another time. Not while he was flying so high.

As if the two men had rehearsed the move, Cameron picked her up exactly as his father had and spun her around.

"We kicked ass at that festival. I wish you could have been there, because, honey, we just—"

"Kicked ass."

He laughed, spun her around once more, then put her down, but not before he'd stolen a kiss that continued long after she was back on planet Earth. By the time they did break apart, everyone in the brewery was either staring at them or pointedly not staring. Cameron rolled his eyes, unconcerned, but she felt her face heat and her heart beat faster.

"Come on. Let's leave these jokers to their work. I've missed you. A hell of a lot."

"I want to hear all about the festival and what you've been doing. It seems like we haven't seen each other in ages."

He sobered a bit, caught and kept her gaze. "I know. I won't lie. It hasn't been easy." Then he took a quick look behind him and led her straight to the exit. Not the one that led to the bar. "You want to come upstairs?"

"Now? I thought—"

"We can go out to dinner if you want," he said. "But Karla's made us something special, which won't be ready until about six-thirty."

"That's so nice. Of course we'll wait."

"Good. I've put in a specific order for no blackouts, no emergencies, no interruptions at all. Before and after we eat." He took her hand as they walked to the staircase. "You can still stay, right?"

"I can. But I have to be up—"

"Before the sun. I figured. Hey, if you want, after we eat we can go back to your place so you can sleep in."

She didn't answer him as they climbed the staircase. It was very likely that she'd never again meet a man as terrific as Cam. He was exceptional in so many ways. She wished she could just be grateful for the brief time she'd had with him, instead of dreading their goodbye.

He'd just set the bar so damn high.

"Iced tea? Soda? Iced coffee?"

The door hadn't even closed behind him yet and he was already making sure she was taken care of. "I'll get the drinks. You tell me about your spectacular wins."

He didn't say anything for a long moment. Just stared at her, the joy that had him practically glowing mere minutes ago dimming with each passing second.

"Cameron, what's wrong?"

"Nothing. I shouldn't… It's nothing. We'll talk about it another time."

"No. That's not fair. You can't leave me wondering. I won't be able to think of anything else."

"It's just…I don't want you to think I was hiding something. And I need you to know so that we can discuss things."

"What things?"

His eyes closed for a moment, then opened again. "I got the call from my boss. We're fully funded."

After a stunned silence, she said, "That's good, right?"

"Right." He gave her a small smile and touched her face. "They want the team to get straight to work. They're making sure we have the best resources money can buy. There's oversight, which is always good, but we're in this for the long haul, with yearly reviews to see if we need more capital. It's not just U.S. funds, either. The World Health Organization has taken a stand, and we're going to be one of four facilities worldwide working on the problem. We'll share information, which is kind of unprecedented, but this isn't about profit. Well, not all about profit."

He'd spoken so quickly, she wasn't sure she'd gotten

all the details, but it didn't matter, because there was only one that counted. He was leaving. "When?"

"Next month."

Her breath left her in a huff. They'd both be leaving in October? That should have made her feel better, but October was too soon. Far too soon. He had his arms around her before she even realized she needed them to hold her up. "Hey, wait. I know it's a long way from here to Syracuse, but maybe I could, you know, come down on weekends. When you had an event or whatever. I can always work on the train. That way you can stay on track with your schedule and I'll try to be there to help when you need me."

She shook her head, but couldn't get her voice to work. He would do that for her?

"I wouldn't get in the way of your career," he said. "I swear to God, I wouldn't. I know how important it is for you, and how busy you are, but—"

She raised her hand and covered his mouth. "Stop. Please. I was going to tell you, but everything happened so fast. I'm going to France."

His forehead furrowed, and she let him speak. "France? When? For how long?"

"I'm leaving at the end of next month. I've been offered a position there. With Phillip and Simone. I'll be working side by side with them at the vineyard and selling wines all over the world."

"Oh. No kidding." He seemed shocked. Of course he was—this had come out of the blue. "That would be a good career move, huh?"

She nodded.

His hold on her loosened and he took a half step back. "That's impressive. And it's with your foster parents, so that's the best, right? That'll put you on the map. You'll be leaps and bounds ahead of the game."

Her insides twisted as what had always been a comfortable silence between them became a wall. "We always
knew this wasn't supposed to be forever," she said finally.
"It wasn't even supposed to be real."

He nodded. But he didn't look at her.

"And, anyway, you're going to be doing the work of a
lifetime. You shouldn't be worrying about traveling on
weekends—you should be resting. Thinking. Making yourself a life in Syracuse. You said you would probably be on
that project for the rest of your career."

"That's…that's true. I will. I've got a down payment
saved to buy a place there. The housing market's decent.
Not like Manhattan, that's for sure."

She wanted to be happy for him. He deserved all the
happiness in the world. How had they let it go so far? After
all her planning and assurances that it was impossible, how
on earth had she not realized she'd fallen in love?

"You know, I think I'll make myself a drink," he said.
"I've got some fine whiskey in the cupboard. A gift from
one of my thesis advisers. He's from Scotland. It's a Talisker,
aged eighteen years." He opened a high cupboard and pulled
out a tall blue box. Before he opened it, he brought down
two glasses. "Would you like some? Or I can still make you
a soda or some iced tea."

"I'd like some whiskey. Thank you. I've never had Talisker,
and I've heard it's great."

"Yeah. I like mine on the rocks."

"Me, too."

He pulled up the bottle, the amber liquid shining in the
light from the setting sun. "They say it's fiery, yet tastes
like it was made from the sea. That's because they make
it on the Isle of Skye right at the beach in Loch Harport."

She smiled. "Think we can ever drink anything without wanting to know its provenance?"

"Soda," he said. "I don't care where my cola comes from."

"That's true."

She rubbed her arms, sorry she'd worn a sleeveless blouse now that she felt so chilly. The clink of ice cubes didn't help much, but the scotch should warm her up.

She should have never talked about France. Not today, not after his victory.

When he finally turned around, he held out her glass. She took it, and he lifted his own. "To your brilliant career."

Her glass kissed his. "To yours."

BEST IDEA HE'D had in ages, pulling out the Talisker. It made it much easier to paste on a smile when they went down to dinner. The whole family, except for Ruby, who'd gone back to Indiana, was gathered there, along with every one of the pub's employees. It was a huge damn party, where they had enough prizewinning beer for only one round each because they'd sold so much at the festival.

Karla had pulled out all the stops. She'd made enough smoked brisket and tamales to feed an army. Her kids had cooked up her special-recipe potato salad, and the bakery two doors down had brought in a giant sheet cake with The Four Sisters logo on top.

The place was more crowded than the night of the blackout, and Cam's back hurt from getting congratulated by so many people. It helped that Molly was trying so hard. She really was happy for him, and except for how monumentally fucked-up everything was, he was happy for her, too.

Soon she'd be with the family she loved, and he'd be with his team. It would be okay. They'd both be busy as hell, and work was so consuming, he'd probably get over her in no time.

They ate, although his appetite wasn't what it could have been, and they lifted their glasses for a number of toasts. And since it seemed to be the night for making announcements, he figured he'd make one more.

He stood up and whistled to get everyone's attention. It took a while, but finally the room was as quiet as it was going to get with a plethora of beer drinkers in it. "I have news, people. October 31, you won't have me to kick around anymore. I'm going back to my real job. The one that doesn't involve a bunch of bikers making a mess every damn night or a jukebox that makes the bed shake like it's got Magic Fingers."

"I heard it wasn't a jukebox making that bed shake."

Cam wasn't sure which idiot had yelled that out, but it got a laugh, and a blush from Molly. "Sorry, sweetie," he said. "I warned you about this place."

"It's fine," she said as she stood. She lifted her glass, filled with draft beer this time. "Here's to the man who created the fantastic beer we all love so much, and who's leaving behind his wonderful family for one of the most important jobs in the world. You watch—before he's through, he's going to save this pitiful world of ours from our own excesses. To Dr. Cameron Crawford."

The cheers barely penetrated. He didn't even remember to take a drink for his own toast. He just kept staring at her. At the woman he was going to miss so much, he could barely comprehend it.

"Hold up," he said, so quietly his father had to repeat it for him in a loud voice. Gordon got everyone to shut up again and then Cam turned to his dad. "Sorry to give you the news like this, but hell, everyone here's family, right? Don't worry. I'll make sure there are plenty of fall and winter beers ready to try before I leave."

His father shook his head as if he didn't give a crap

about the beer. "I'm glad you got the funding, son. I'm proud of you, and I always will be."

A smattering of applause died down quickly as Cam looked at each one of his sisters. "You've been a real pain in my ass."

"Ah, stop," Amber said. "You know we hate it when you get all mushy."

He smiled as best he could. "There's one last surprise for tonight." He turned toward Emmy, standing at the edge of the bar. "Would you mind?"

"No worries, bro. I kind of figured." She disappeared into the kitchen, but came out again just after he'd put his glass down, holding five bottles of beer. She handed one to Cam. He walked over to Molly.

The folks behind the bar stepped back some, and the folks on the other side pushed closer. "I made this for you, Molly Grainger. It's going to be on tap here at The Four Sisters. One of our year-round selections."

Molly took the bottle and held it as if it were made of diamonds. "It's got my name on it," she said. Her voice was so soft that he barely heard her.

"I know," he said.

"Molly's Dark Ale for Wine Lovers."

"I know," he said, and he couldn't be sad, not when her eyes were brimming with tears and she looked so stunned.

"This is the most amazing thing I've ever—" Her voice faltered.

"Why don't you hold that thought until you taste it."

The few people close enough to hear laughed, and then a hushed murmur fell across the room.

He took the ice-cold bottle, popped the top and handed it back to her. His heart was beating a mile a minute and he was more invested in her liking this beer than he was in getting gold medals.

She sipped. Took another bigger sip. Then smiled so

big, it was as though she'd invented the move. "This beer is gorgeous," she said. "It's like the very best things about beer met the very best parts of Cabernet Sauvignon and they got married and had kids."

Cam closed his eyes as his chin dropped to his chest. Okay. That settled it. He'd pick up his sorrows later. Because Molly was still his tonight.

19

MOLLY LOOKED AT the time again. She knew Phillip and Simone were scheduled to leave in the morning, but they hadn't spoken since the afternoon they'd taken her to lunch. She had too many unanswered questions and she didn't relish trying to speak to Phillip once he was back in Bordeaux.

She'd waited until four to call. They usually didn't have cocktails until six. Besides, Cameron was coming over in an hour, and she wanted this done with so she wouldn't be distracted. Phillip's phone rang several times, and she was prepared to leave a message when he finally picked up. "Hello, Molly. We were just on our way out. Can this wait?"

"Not really. I shouldn't keep you for long, but I need some information."

He called out to Simone that he'd be a few minutes. "What do you need?"

"Travel arrangements, primarily."

"Ah, yes. Mathilde was to have called you with the details yesterday. A situation arose that she had to take care of."

"Mathilde?"

"She and her husband, Julien, are our personal assis-
tants. You'll meet them soon, of course. Mathilde will help
you find an apartment, probably sharing with one of the
staff. Something near the office. She'll also help you with
your work visa.... Excuse me."

The phone sounded as if he'd put it against his shirt.
The scratching of fabric was loud enough that she couldn't
hear what was being said. It gave her a chance to process
what he'd told her. She shouldn't feel surprised that they
were seeing to her living quarters. There was absolutely no
reason she should've expected she'd be staying with them.
And she hadn't, not really. So why did it hurt?

"Also, we'd like you to come on the twenty-fourth, if at
all possible. We're leaving on the twenty-third for Greece,
but the earlier arrival will give you time to get your things
in order before we return. Ah, Simone has assured me that
Mathilde will call you in ten minutes. Don't worry. She'll
take care of your flight, and Julien will meet you at the
airport and get you settled in the hotel. You'll like it. We
use the same one for all our employees. Travel safely. Now
I must go. We're already late."

"But—" She couldn't seem to catch her breath. "All your
employees?" she repeated, her voice smaller than small.

"Molly? I'm sorry I don't have time—" His impatient
tone brought her around.

So he'd said what he meant.

"Of course.... I'm sorry. I'll wait to hear from Mathilde."

She ended the call, her fingers shaking. What she'd pictured about her new life and what she'd just heard were
miles—no, continents—apart. Sure, Phillip and Simone
had a large estate, but she was no longer their ward. She
was a grown woman. They probably thought she'd want
her own place. But she'd be sharing an apartment. Okay,

fine...what she really hadn't expected was that they'd view her as an employee.

It was the truth, though. There were no blood ties between them, and Phillip and Simone had never been sentimental. Honestly, she was amazingly lucky to get the offer in the first place. Nothing she could have garnered for herself would help her career more. She should be grateful. She swallowed hard, but the lump in her throat wouldn't go away.

God. She needed to get past this. It was a disappointment. Like hundreds of others before it. But it was also an opportunity if she stepped up to the challenge.

She needed to get organized.

The first item on her to-do list was to wrap up her whole life in a month without burning any bridges. She'd notified NYU so they could find a replacement to teach her classes for the rest of the term. Everyone at the radio station already knew and had been gratifyingly sad that she was leaving. Donna had assured her she would be able to continue writing her column for *Wine Connoisseur,* which she was happy about. But there were still so many other things left to do. She had yet to give notice on her apartment, arrange for the shipping of her belongings, connect with all of the event organizers to cancel her appearances... and the list went on.

But all of that was nothing compared to saying goodbye to Cameron.

The phone call from Mathilde interrupted her thoughts, but it wasn't a particularly long conversation. The woman was all business, and Molly learned far more from her than from Phillip. Mathilde told her that Phillip and Simone would cover the cost of shipping her things over. She also told her what her salary would be, which, while not a fortune, would allow her to live well. Finally, Mathilde mentioned that Molly would be traveling quite a bit and entertaining clients. That was something she hadn't even considered, and it left her with a feeling of dread. Especially because she'd be doing it without Cam at her side.

The buzzer rang, followed so quickly by a knock at her door that whoever was there must have run up the stairs. The moment she opened the door and saw Cam, she fell into his arms.

"Hey, what's going on?" he asked, his voice as soft as the hand that petted her hair.

"I'm leaving soon," she said, feeling ridiculous. She wasn't a child, and yet the comfort of his embrace felt as necessary as her heartbeat.

"I know. I hate it, but I know."

She looked up into his dark eyes. "No. I'm leaving a week earlier than I thought."

He inhaled and held it. Finally he smiled, although it wasn't particularly convincing. "Wow, seems fast all of a sudden."

She nodded. "Come in," she said, stepping out of his arms into the apartment. "Sorry. What can I get you? I have the most fantastic beer in the fridge. It's for wine lovers."

His smile became real, but also bittersweet. "How about I just take a soda, and we go lie down."

"It's just after five."

He nodded. "Unless you're hungry."

"Ugh." She shook her head on the way to the refrigerator. "I don't think I could eat anything at the moment."

"Then we'll order something later. Or go out."

She got them both sodas. "Sure. Whatever."

She'd thrown on one of her summer shifts, and he was in jeans and a plain white tee. It would have been easy to strip down, but that wasn't what she wanted. After putting the drinks by the bed, he joined her on top of the sheets and held her tightly against him.

"Having second thoughts?" he asked.

"No. Maybe." She sighed. "I found out I'll be doing a lot of entertaining, dinner with clients, that sort of thing."

"Ah." He kissed her hair. "You'll do great. Look how far you've come. Selling wine at the pub like you're a pro and giving my sisters grief."

"That's different. They're family." Her breath caught when she realized what she'd said. Of course, she didn't mean they were her family.

Bless Cam, he didn't say a word. Just continued to hold her while she closed her eyes and tried to memorize everything about the moment. The way his chest was so firm and yet felt better than any pillow. How his long arms wrapped around her as if he would always keep her safe. How they'd found the perfect way to entwine their legs, as if they were made to fit together.

She couldn't hear his beating heart because of the noise coming from the air conditioner, but she could imagine it, and that would have to do.

"Something else is bothering you. Tell me what happened," he said.

"Turns out I'm an employee." She kept her head down, not wanting him to see her face, read the sadness that was too close to the surface.

"I don't know what that means."

"The irony is," she said, "I never knew what a real family was until I met yours. That sounds crazy, but it's true. I didn't know many people who were outside of the foster system growing up. I used to think that TV families were nonsense. Make-believe." She paused for a breath. "It's okay, though. Phillip and Simone like me. And they believe in my potential. What they've offered me is the opportunity of a lifetime. But they're not family."

"You wanted them to be."

She nodded, tears filling her eyes. "I did."

"I think Simone and Phillip love you, though. I can't imagine anyone knowing you and not loving you."

Her own smile couldn't even reach bittersweet. "I'm grateful to know there are families like yours, even if I never have one of my own. It's nice to think there are kids who grow up like you."

He gave her a squeeze, but didn't say anything for a while. "You know," he said finally, his voice deep and thoughtful. "There are big pharmaceutical firms in Europe. In France, in fact."

She laughed a little. "You know French?"

"No, but I could learn. I've got great credentials. You know MIT is still the top-rated school in the world, especially in the sciences."

Oh, how she loved him right this minute. She'd loved him before, but now the feeling engulfed her completely. Tears spilled from her eyes, and her heart tightened so hard, it was difficult to breathe. "Would you still be working on the antibiotic-resistance problem?"

"Maybe."

His hesitation said all she needed to know. "I love that you suggested it. Thank you. But no. This is your dream come true, and I wouldn't take that away for the world."

Another squeeze was followed by a gentle hand rubbing her back. Oddly, she wasn't in any rush to make love to him, although she was sure they would later. Right now, though, felt like a perfect moment. One she'd think about for years to come. The way he cared for her was so complete. It was about the sex, the laughter, the work, their chemistry and so much more.

He kissed the top of her head. "I love you, too," he whispered.

And there it was. The dream she'd never dared to have had just come true. She was loved by the best man she'd ever met. Unconditionally.

"KNOCK, KNOCK."

Cameron looked up from his packing box to find Emmy at his door. "If you're here to talk about Molly, don't bother. I told you, we've discussed our options."

"Once again, Dr. Smarty-Pants, you are being a dope."

"Because I'm supportive of Molly fulfilling her goals and having the life she's always dreamed of?"

Emmy stepped inside and sat on the bed, facing him. "Because you're not fighting hard enough. You've finally found the magic chemistry you've been waiting for all your life and you're letting her get away. You two are stupidly in love. It's completely obvious. It's everything you've ever believed in."

"Not quite," he said. "This situation is far messier than any formula I could have ever conceived."

"Welcome to the real world. It's always messy. But slogging through that mess is what makes all the difference."

"Or, in some cases, there isn't a happy ending and all you're left with is pain. Look at Dad."

Emmy turned her head for a minute before she said, "Dad isn't a very good example. I don't want to burst your bubble, but he's a dope, too. His marriage to Mom was good, but he's made it into something sacred. It wasn't. They argued—she hated that he spent so much time at the bar. She didn't even like living in New York. Her dream was to move to the Midwest somewhere and have a big house where her kids could have land to play on and she could grow her own vegetables."

"What?"

"Ruby's old enough to remember the real thing, not the stories, and the two of us shared a bedroom for a long time. Don't memorialize Molly. Think about how much she means to you. What it might take to keep her."

He looked at his half-filled box of books. "I offered to try to find a job in France."

"Good for you. Now try harder."

He didn't know his sister had left until he looked up twenty minutes later.

HER PLANE WAS leaving in one hour and eight minutes. If she caught a cab right this second, she'd make it by the skin of her teeth.

Instead, she reached for the door of The Four Sisters brewpub.

How she'd ended up here, she wasn't sure. She could have gone to Donna's. Or to France. But no. She'd come to Sunnyside Gardens, Queens. Odd. Especially considering Cameron was in Syracuse for the night. Because of her. Because she'd told him she'd never be able to leave if he'd come to the airport. Because he couldn't stand the idea of being in town when she took off from LaGuardia.

She could have saved him a long trip.

Her belongings had been sent in stages, with the last shipment going out early this morning, to be delivered in Bordeaux in five days. All she had with her now was a well-stuffed carry-on. That was it. Nothing else.

The pub wasn't terribly crowded for a Friday. The music wasn't even pounding. There were a few empty seats at the bar, but she didn't recognize the bartender. It was the first time she'd been here when there hadn't been at least three people behind the bar.

"What can I get you?"

"Do you have Molly's Dark Ale on tap?"

"We do. One second."

She folded her hands on the cool mahogany counter-top and studied them so she had something to do. When her draft came, it wasn't the new guy who brought it over.

"Gordon."

"Cam's not here, sweetheart."

"I know." She shrugged. "I'm not even sure why I'm here."

He picked up her glass again and said, "Come on. Let's go someplace a little more private. Have ourselves a talk."

Her purse in one hand, her luggage in the other, she followed him through the kitchen to his office. He settled down in his big old rolling chair while she took one on the other side of the desk.

"I imagine this week has been pretty hectic."

"You have no idea. I don't think I've slept for more than four hours in the last seven days."

"France is far away. It's a big move. I can't imagine the decision to go was easy."

She sipped her beer, thankful beyond words Gordon had assumed she'd missed her flight. "It's been the hardest decision of my life."

"So Cam's said. He's very proud of you."

"Of me?" She dismissed the remark with a shake of her head. "He's one to talk. He's amazing. Brilliant. The whole world should be thrilled that he's working on something this important."

"Well, the world as far as we know it is. But I'm wondering if it's worth the sacrifice. Not just for him, either."

Before she could even think of hiding them, tears welled in her eyes and fell. "I can't turn down this job. It's what I've worked for since I was sixteen. Everything I own is on a ship. I've given up all my jobs. And he certainly can't give up his work. He already told me it was the most important thing he'd ever done."

Gordon got up and took the chair next to her, moving it close enough for him to put his arm over her shoulders. "For what it's worth," he said, "I'd have been so proud and happy if you were my daughter. No matter what you do. You're a wonderful girl, Molly. Wonderful."

That was it for her. She was getting his T-shirt all wet, but he never let go of her. Not until the well ran dry.

"Do you want help getting another flight?" he asked, when she'd finally finished off the last tissue.

She shook her head without hesitation.

"All right. How about you get some sleep, huh? Tomorrow things will be a lot clearer."

She picked up her carry-on and followed him upstairs to Cameron's apartment. Once she was inside, he kissed her forehead good-night before locking the door behind him.

CAMERON CLIMBED OUT of the taxi in front of the pub. He was exhausted. He hadn't had a breather since he'd gotten on the early train for Syracuse. Once there, he'd met with a Realtor and seen a half dozen great-looking condos, duplexes and town houses, only to realize he wanted a house with a yard and a big kitchen, a barbecue outside, a couple of extra bedrooms for whoever might come over. It would have to be a fixer-upper, but that worked for him. He didn't want to have any spare time to think.

Molly was gone. Really gone. On a plane halfway to Bordeaux.

If he'd had any working brain cells left he would've stayed in Syracuse overnight. The train trip home had been even more tiring than searching for a place to live, if that was possible. Instead of sleeping, which he'd meant to do, he'd worked on a problem that had no apparent answer. He'd come up with solutions to impossible problems before, so he couldn't let it go untested.

Sadly, no magic solution had appeared, but at least he'd tried. And he'd continue to try, because he was built for hope.

The stairs up to his apartment, however, seemed insurmountable. But he climbed them before someone walked out of the bar and ambushed him. He doubted he could be pleasant.

Of course, his key stuck in the lock and he had to jiggle it. The instant he opened the door he swore he could smell her. Talk about fate being cruel.

He automatically reached for the light switch before he realized he'd obviously left the lamp on. He froze at the threshold and blinked. "Molly?"

She was on his bed. Sitting there, looking at him. It was midnight, her flight had left hours ago, and yet here she was. Wearing his New York Jets jersey. Eyes puffy and red. Smiling.

"Hi," she said.

He dropped his duffel bag with a thunk. "What happened? Did you miss your flight? Is it delayed?"

"Nope. You look like you could use some sleep."

"I would have agreed a minute ago," he said. "But I seem to have found a second wind."

She stood, pressed her lips together, clenched her fists and released them, only to clench them again.

In four steps he was in front of her and pulling her close until they were pressed against each other. First he kissed her because he could. A long, sweet kiss that settled him like no pill or drink ever could. Finally, when he could stand to part, he said, "What's going on?"

"I'm not going to France."

He didn't know what to say at first, though she looked serious enough.

"Today?" he asked cautiously. "Or ever?"

She smiled and used her thumb to soothe the wrinkle that must have been between his eyebrows. "Well, if I ever have the money I'd like to visit someday."

"You're telling me you're staying. Here. In New York."

She nodded. "Unfortunately, all my belongings are already on their way."

"Oh. Okay. Uh, how about we both sit down?"

"Yes, I think so." She settled back onto the bed and he pulled up a chair in front of her. Close enough to reach over and touch her.

"Are you sure about this?" If Cam was dreaming, he'd be really pissed later. He closed his hand over her soft warm flesh. "You seem sure. But you seem nervous, too."

"Um, when I said all of my belongings are gone, I wasn't joking. And of course, I have no apartment. No job to speak of. I can still count on Donna and the magazine, but that's all."

Her words slowly sank in. That foundation she'd built to keep her safe? All gone. But here she was, looking less freaked-out than he was. His heart was ready to explode. God. Molly was staying…. Her hand moved beneath his and he saw he was squeezing too hard.

"I didn't know anything about wine until I met Phillip and Simone," she said. "I didn't know you could get a degree in enology or a master of wine or even what a sommelier was.

"And I now have two of those, with one coming next year, all because of my own efforts. I even have the student loans to prove it. The point is, though I learned a great deal from them, I did the work that got me where I am. I've been supporting myself since I went away to college, and I work hard to pay off my debts. But I always manage."

"Smart, determined, brave and beautiful," he said. "I

can't see a single thing that will stop you from achieving all your goals."

She nodded, her lips pressed together. "Yes," she said. "I will. Whether the journey is by jet or by train, I'll get there in the end, because I can. I know it."

Something stirred in his chest that he didn't want to acknowledge. He might be built for hope, but he wasn't a fool. "You're not afraid to start over?"

"Of course I am. But I'm more afraid of not having a *life*. Donna warned me, and she was right. I never let myself dream that I could have more than a career, but now…"

He leaned forward, needing to read her as well as he possibly could. "Tell me what you mean. Please."

"I can't give this up, Cam. I can't. I would regret it forever. I hope you still want me." She was on the verge of tears and he was close himself.

He cupped his hand around the back of her neck. "Oh, honey—"

"I mean, your family. I barely know them, and I feel more affection for your father and sisters than I have for anyone except for Donna. And then there's you, of course."

"Yeah, always the afterthought."

She smiled. "Never. Not since the night we met." She pulled him over to the bed. They turned so they were touching knees, close enough that she could sink into the comfort of his scent and the depths of his eyes. "I fell in love with you. That's not supposed to happen with a one-night stand. I was right to be worried about you being a distraction."

"I wish I could say I was sorry about that, but I'm not. You know I feel the same. You're the woman I've been waiting for all my life. But the last thing I wanted to do was derail your dreams. I fell in love with exactly who you are, with all that drive and energy and determination. I want the best for you. Always. Even if that means I need to stand back."

"I know. And that's exactly why I can stay. Why I know this is where I belong. I'm not willing to settle for being the number one wine critic in the world. That's not enough. That's half a life. You and me together. That completes the picture."

She kissed him. A sweet kiss with a dash of sass as she nipped his bottom lip before she pulled back. "I want the same for you, Cam. You belong with your team in Syracuse, and I think I might have thought of a way to make everything possible."

She hopped off the bed and went to one of his packing boxes. She pulled out his big atlas of America and brought it back to the bed and laid it in front of him.

"That's Syracuse," she said, pointing to the top of the map of greater New York. "And that's the East Village, which I'm using as a central point because most of my work is there—or I should say, will be there." She moved her finger to Queens. "This is the apartment. Why are you smiling like that?"

"You're so...organized."

"And you're surprised?"

Cam shook his head. "Turned on. Please continue," he said and nuzzled the spot behind her ear.

"You can't do that and pay attention at the same time. My plan won't necessarily be inexpensive or easy."

"Don't care. You're here." He bit her earlobe. "We'll make it work."

"Wait," she said, laughing. "Scranton, Pennsylvania, is 138 miles from right here, 130 miles from Syracuse."

He reared back. "Scranton?"

"See? I told you—"

"I'm kidding. I know what you're saying. I already

thought of it myself. We'd have this apartment, find a place in Scranton and I get an inexpensive place in Syracuse—"

"Yes! Sometimes I'd have to stay close to Manhattan, and sometimes you'd work too late or what have you. We wouldn't see each other every day, of course, but we'd manage. Because both of us can work on the train. It wouldn't be lost time." She paused. "When did you think of this?"

"Last week," he admitted and shrugged. "I was a drowning man looking for a lifeline."

"Don't you dare make me cry."

"Fine. I'll be the only one, then," he said, brushing the hair off her face.

Molly sighed. "What do you think, Dr. Crawford?"

"I think I looked for houses in the wrong place."

Her forehead furrowed. "I made a big assumption about this place, though."

"Believe me. The family's going to be so happy, they'd give us Dad's house if it meant we stay together."

"That's…" She sniffed. "You weren't supposed to make me cry."

"Happy tears are allowed, I think," he said, his gaze intent on hers. "This is going to work. You know that?"

She nodded.

"I love you, you brilliant woman."

"I love you, too, you brilliant man." She pulled him down on top of her, and his kiss was the first of their brand-new life together.

* * * * *

REQUEST YOUR FREE BOOKS!
2 FREE NOVELS PLUS 2 FREE GIFTS!

HARLEQUIN

Blaze®

red-hot reads!

HBI3R2

Entering her building, Lara felt the weight of the day on her shoulders. She still had hours of homework and eight shows to dance over the weekend. If she nailed this assignment, she'd have the top grade in the class, which meant an internship with a top-flight security firm.

Six more weeks to go. With a sigh, she rounded the hallway to her corridor.

Lara Lee, Cyber Detective.

She grinned, then blinked. Frowning, she noted the hall lighting was out. She'd just put her key in the lock when she felt him.

It wasn't his body heat that tipped her off.

Nope, it was the lust swirling through her system, making her knees weak and her nipples ache.

Taking a deep breath, she turned. "Do you always lurk in the shadows?"

"Hall light is out. Shadows are all you've got here."

"What do you want?"

"I told you. I need to talk to you about your brother."

"And I told you. I don't have a brother."

Not anymore.

"Lieutenant Phillip Banks. Navy SEAL. Ring any bells?" His words were easy, the look in his eyes as mellow as the half smile on his full lips.

"My last name is Lee." Then, before she could stop herself, she asked, "Why are you running errands for this guy, anyway?"

His dark eyes flashed. "Sweetheart, do I look like anyone's errand boy?" he said.

Lara couldn't resist.

She let her eyes wander down the long, hard length of his body. Broad shoulders and a drool-worthy chest tapered into flat abs, narrow hips and strong thighs.

She wet her lips and met his eyes again.

He looked hot.

As if he'd like to strip her down and play show-and-tell.

Tempting, since she'd bet that'd would be worth seeing.

"Sorry," she said. "I'm not the woman you're looking for."

Damn.

Not for the first time in his life, Dominic Castillo cursed Banks. The guy was a pain. Figured that long, lean and sexy was just as bad.

He wanted to grab her, haul her off to the nearest horizontal surface.

Insane.

He was on a mission. *She* was his duty.

He'd never lusted after a mission before.

Pick up A SEAL'S FANTASY by Tawny Weber, available in September 2014 wherever you buy Harlequin® Blaze® books.

Can They Take the Heat?

On a cruise, fashion blogger Carly Pendleton tries to fight her attraction to "Average Joe" contest winner Joe Tedesco, who sizzles with raw masculinity. They don't seem to have much in common...but can she fight the fire blazing between them?

From the reader-favorite ***The Wrong Bed*** miniseries

Cabin Fever
by *Jillian Burns*

Available September 2014 wherever you buy Harlequin Blaze books.

♦HARLEQUIN®

Blaze®

Red-Hot Reads
www.Harlequin.com

HARLEQUIN®

A *Romance* FOR EVERY MOOD™

Stay up-to-date on all your
romance-reading news with the
Harlequin Shopping Guide,
featuring bestselling authors, exciting new
miniseries, books to watch and more!

The newest issue will be delivered right to you
with our compliments! There are 4 each year.

Signing up is easy.

EMAIL

ShoppingGuide@Harlequin.ca

WRITE TO US

HARLEQUIN BOOKS
Attention: Customer Service Department
P.O. Box 9057, Buffalo, NY 14269-9057

OR PHONE

1-800-873-8635 in the United States
1-888-343-9777 in Canada

Please allow 4-6 weeks for delivery of the first issue by mail.